The Christmas Husband Hunt

Books by Kate Moore

The Husband Hunter's Guide to London
A Lady's Guide to Passion and Property
A Spy's Guide to Seduction
The Christmas Husband Hunt

The Christmas Husband Hunt

Kate Moore

LYRICAL PRESS
Kensington Publishing Corp.
www.kensingtonbooks.com

First Electronic Edition: November 2019
eISBN-13: 978-1-5161-0999-9
eISBN-10: 1-5161-0999-6

First Print Edition: November 2019
ISBN-13: 978-1-5161-1000-1
ISBN-10: 1-5161-1000-5

Printed in the United States of America

To my siblings and fellow stocking-hangers—Ned, Nancy, Joan, Sarah, and Kim—may Christmas always bring you joy!

"A governess is almost shut out of society; not choosing to associate with servants, and not being treated as an equal by the heads of the house or their visitors, she must possess some fortitude and strength of mind to render herself tranquil or happy..."

—Nelly Weeton, Letter to Mrs. Dodson, 18 August 1821

from Hall, E. (ed) 1936 *Miss Weeton: Journal of a Governess 1811-1825 (London)*

Author's Note

The common view holds that Christmas was not much celebrated in England before Prince Albert introduced the Christmas tree and Charles Dickens wrote *A Christmas Carol.* Yet the letters of Jane Austen and her family, her novels, and the diaries of obscure country parsons tell of the gatherings, games, and feasts of the eighteenth and early nineteenth centuries. From King Arthur's time to Shakespeare's the Twelve Days of Christmas were kept with song and dance, green boughs, and cakes with hidden treasures in them.

Christmas in Austen's time was in fact much anticipated and prepared for—not with Black Friday sales, but with fattening of the animals that would make the feast and a day set aside for making the pudding. There were masquerades and acts of charity. Children received Christmas boxes of coins. On St. Stephen's Day (when King Wenceslas looked out, as the carol says), or Boxing Day as it's now called, people went for a hike or a walk. Rustic musicians called Waits, once officially sanctioned and later banned, took their carols to the streets of London. Vendors drove holly carts through the city. There was a Yule log and a Yule candle, and of course, there was mistletoe, though not in some churches, where it was shunned as a practice of the Druids.

So as you read *The Christmas Husband Hunt,* I hope it brings the ancient spirit of Christmas alive again in your heart.

Now Christmas is come,
Let us beat up the drum
And call all our neighbors together;
And when they appear,
Let us make them such cheer,
As will keep out the wind and the weather.

The advantages of the single state are best enjoyed by young men of fortune, birth, and personal attraction.

—The Husband Hunter's Guide to London

Chapter 1

"Are we finished?" Charles Davenham asked, one dark brow raised. He stood in black evening wear before a cheval glass in his dressing room, enduring the satisfied scrutiny of his friend Peregrine Pilkington and a severe, brow-knitting frown from Oxley, his valet. Perry had added an alarming number of items to Charles's ensemble and now considered the effect of an emerald stickpin in the flowing folds of Charles's neckcloth.

The candles flickered in a slight draft, and Charles recalled the open window over the desk in his bedroom. Outside, the wind was rising for the first gale of the season. It would pour soon, and he preferred to get to his quarry before the skies opened.

"Perry, you are enjoying this too much." It was Perry who had come up with the idea of the extravagant waistcoats as a disguise.

"Am I?" Perry asked.

A row of fobs and seals dangled from the rather exotic persimmon-colored waistcoat Perry had insisted Charles wear. "I'll jingle like sleigh bells when I walk."

"The point is, dear boy, to distract the marchioness with your finery—rings and farthingales and things." Perry circled a fine, thin hand in the air. "Besides, it's your fault we have to rely on sparklers. You've too much muscle on you. Can't disguise your shoulders."

"I asked you here for your help with the woman's family tree. You're the expert in aunts, uncles, and third cousins once-removed. I'm counting on you to spot any flaw in the lady's credentials."

Oxley, who had voiced no disapproval of Charles's sartorial choices for nearly a decade, shuddered and turned away from the waistcoat with a tray of jewels Perry had earlier rejected.

Perry stopped him. "Rings. We need rings."

With a sigh, Oxley held out the tray.

Charles groaned.

"You think the marchioness is the one the Foreign Office is after?" Perry asked, holding out two rings—a cabochon ruby and a square-cut diamond.

"Who else?" Charles slid the rings onto the fingers of his right hand. They had belonged to his father, but Charles had worn only the signet he inherited with the title, Viscount Wynford.

"Are you going to expose her at midnight? The way a masquerade ball ends when the hostess invites everyone to tear away his disguise?"

Charles shook his head. "I can't act without proof. Look at her family tree again, Perry, and tell me whether there's any chance the woman is who she claims to be."

Perry picked up a piece of yellowing parchment from a side table. "The thing is in bleeding French. How am I supposed to tell one frog from another?"

"Tell me where the likely forgery is, and we'll investigate further." By we, Charles meant his fellow analysts working for the Foreign Office.

Charles turned from the mirror to look over Perry's shoulder at the document, a page torn from a Bible. It had just come into his hands, and he was eager to see whether it shed any light on the marchioness's past. She might be who she claimed to be, a distant cousin of Charles's late mother, now restored to her lands and titles in post-Napoleonic France. Or she could be, as he and two Foreign Office colleagues suspected, a Russian spy borrowing a lapsed identity to position herself in London society to receive and pass along the government's secrets to the Russian agent Zovsky in Paris.

Ever since Napoleon's fall, Russia and England had been circling like two pugilists in a ring, measuring each other's reach and power. Each country had agents in the other's capital. Russian agents, trained in deception, trolled the political and social waters of London in search of weak, indebted, or unprincipled members of fashionable society who could be persuaded to offer secrets to the Russians for a price.

In the spring, British counteragents had made a small crack in a ring of spies that had been operating in London for some time. With the arrest of the popular émigré Count Malikov and the death of his chief courier, Sir Geoffrey Radcliffe, they had slowed the flow of information to the Russians. No one in the Foreign Office, however, doubted the Russians would try again, and when Malikov died in prison under suspicious circumstances, and the French marchioness appeared claiming to be related to Charles, it had been natural for Lord Chartwell of the Foreign Office to approach Charles for the mission of exposing her. It would be his first mission in the field.

The timing was not ideal, as Charles knew he could count on Perry to remind him.

"So if you don't expose the marchioness tonight, you won't go home for Christmas," Perry said, holding the document closer to the light.

"Can't," Charles insisted. "Not when we're so close to cracking the spy ring."

Perry frowned and lowered the parchment back to the table. The writing was small, the ink faint, and the document much amended with dates added for marriages and deaths.

Charles could see Perry's eyes in rapid motion, a sign his friend's nimble brain was at work. In Charles's opinion, Perry's parents had a great deal to answer for in the upbringing of their only son, starting with his christening. One did not name a boy Peregrine Pilkington and then send him at the tender age of eight to an English public school, no matter how ancient his pedigree or how fat his papa's wallet. A brilliant student, Perry had refused to fight any of the aristocratic ruffians who had mocked him mercilessly. It was Charles who had developed a punishing left hook in the service of his friend's honor. It was what he did. He protected. He couldn't help it. He'd been protecting Octavia ever since he'd cradled her in his arms under a reeking pile of fishing nets on the French beach where rogue soldiers of the great nation had murdered their mother.

Charles's sister, Octavia, now twenty, was the one reason he might be persuaded to postpone his pursuit of the marchioness. He never missed Christmas at home with his sister. It was a pact he'd made long ago and never broken. He and Octavia even had a name for their particular form of the annual holiday. In an unguarded moment, he'd confided as much to Perry.

Charles wasn't sure exactly why Christmas always seemed so flat at Wynford Hall, but it did. Perhaps it was the vicar with his objection to merriment of any kind and specifically to mistletoe, which he tried to ban from all the neighboring houses as a druidical practice inconsistent with proper English worship.

Charles thought the absence this year of an elder brother might make Christmas easier for Octavia to endure. The family's neighbors, the Greshams, whose son Horace had been a third party to many of Charles's and Octavia's Yuletide adventures, had extended their usual invitation to the season's festivities.

Perry straightened and tapped a line of the marchioness's family tree. "If there's a weakness in the lady's pedigree, I'd say it's right here. According to this tree, your marchioness shares a great-grandparent with you. If the fourth earl's daughter, who married into the Delatour family, had a son who lost his life in the Terror, then your marchioness is your second cousin. See this line here."

Charles looked at the tiny notation of a row of siblings born some fifty years earlier in the French town of Saumur.

Perry tapped the page. "If Great Uncle Victor is legitimate, then the marchioness is indeed your cousin and the widow of the deceased Marquis de Tonnelier." He paused. "But that's the thing about a family tree. You can add an extra twig if no one's alive to dispute the fiction."

That was the rub. The revolution's zeal to erase the past had led to the loss of many of the records families relied on to establish claims to their former estates.

Charles looked at the line of offspring Perry had pointed out, a generation of French nobles who had passed away before the Revolution. Their children and most of their children's children had perished in the Terror. According to the marchioness, her late father-in-law had sent key documents to England for safekeeping when King Louis was first arrested. Now, she—Isabelle Delatour, Marchioness de Tonnelier—claimed to be the sole survivor of two ancient families.

"Thanks, Perry. We'll look into Great Uncle Victor." Charles straightened. His fobs jingled. It was time to face the marchioness. It surprised him how easily her claim to be a cousin, a remnant of his mother's past, brought back that past, his summers in the vineyards of Saumur, and that last day in France.

As he tugged the appalling waistcoat into place and Oxley held out his hat and gloves, the door to his dressing room blew open, banging against the paneled wall. Shouts rose from the entry below.

"Someone's opened the front door, my lord," Oxley said.

"Sounds like your sister's voice," Perry said.

Charles heard it too, unmistakably Octavia's voice, raised in distress. He strode for the stairs. His sister could not be in London. His sister never left Wynford Hall.

From the top of the stairs he looked down on an odd tableau: Octavia in a soaked and muddied cloak, clutching a small traveling case and confronting a London jarvey in a slouched hat and sopping greatcoat.

"Well, I won't pay you that ridiculous sum. You're trying to gammon me because you think I'm a flat. You'd never try such stuff on my brother." His sister turned to look up the stairs. "Charles, come sort this jarvey."

"Now, miss," the man began, "I b'aint askin' too much. Bein' out in a storm, taking yer extra bags, comin' clear 'cross Lunnon at this hour. Think of me poor 'orse, for pity's sake."

"Oh," said Octavia, her shoulders slumping. "I never thought of the poor animal." She struggled with the strings of her reticule. Then her head came up again. "Your horse is no excuse to keep my bags from me. You just think I'm good for more blunt. You're a low, wretched, wretched..."

"*Extortioner*, I believe is the word you're looking for, Octavia." Charles reached the bottom of the stairs. The door remained open, a stiff breeze blowing rain across the black and white tiled floor. Pratt, Charles's butler, appeared frozen in place.

"Charles!" Octavia turned and flung herself into his arms, a shaking bundle of wet wool. Over her head, Charles signaled Pratt to settle with the jarvey. The two men turned away.

Against his shoulder Octavia poured out a tale of a horrid journey by stage.

"The stage? Octavia, where's Nurse? Who knows you left Wynford?"

Octavia stiffened in his arms. She pulled back. "Oh, I'm sorry. You're going out, and I've made you..." Her eyes widened as she took in the persimmon waistcoat. "... all wet. Is that what gentlemen of fashion wear in London?"

"No. It's what Perry made me wear. Only for tonight. But I won't be going out."

"Is it for a wager, then?"

"No. Why the stage, Octavia?"

She drew herself up. Her cheeks were pale, her nose red, and her eyes over-bright. If he didn't know his sweet-eating sister as well as he did, he would say she'd lost half a stone.

"Don't worry, Charles. I won't be any trouble to you. I just need a place to stay while I find a husband."

"A husband?" Charles and Perry spoke as one, and Charles realized his friend had come down to stand beside him.

Octavia nodded vigorously, sending water flying from her bonnet. "You must have a friend who needs a wife, Charles?"

Perry took a step back.

Octavia turned to Perry. "Oh, hello, Peregrine. Don't worry. I didn't mean you."

"But Octavia," Charles said, "right now I'm in the middle of—"

Perry nudged him. "He's in the middle of the single life. That's what he's in the middle of, and that's no place for a young lady."

Octavia tilted her head to one side, regarding them both with suspicion. "I thought gentlemen sought young ladies to marry. My book says..." She lowered the case she was carrying to the floor.

"Octavia, surely you want a Season. In the spring, we can..." He cast a look of desperate appeal at Perry.

"Harry Swanley," Perry announced decisively.

Octavia beamed. "You see, Charles. Perry knows someone."

Perry shook his head. "No, not that sort of Harry. Meant to say Lady Harriet. She's a fourth cousin on your father's side. She's just the person to take Octavia to all the right dinners and balls."

"Oh, no need." Octavia dropped to her knees on the wet, muddied floor and began to rummage through her bag.

"Harriet Swanley?" Charles asked Perry. He knew Lionel Swanley, Lord Dunraven, and had a profound distaste for the man.

"Oh, she's nothing like Dunraven," said Perry. "Hasn't lived with him for years. Lives with the Luxboroughs. Never married. You can call on her tomorrow. I'm sure she'd be glad to help Octavia."

Octavia straightened from her case, holding up a small blue book with gold filigree lettering, *The Husband Hunter's Guide to London.* "No need to call on Lady Harriet, Charles. I've read this book from cover to cover. I know just what to do to get a husband by Christmas."

Charles looked at his sister's thin, pale cheeks and over-bright eyes.

"Lady Harry." Perry insisted.

"I'll call on her in the morning." Charles recognized that he needed help. The over-bright glitter in his sister's eyes came not from a danger one could fight, but from something outside an older brother's experience. The marchioness would have to wait to get an eyeful of his persimmon waistcoat.

It must be said that not every husband hunter will have that combination of sense, character, and good fortune that preserves her from unwise attachments until she meets a man she can both love and respect. Indeed, it falls to the lot of many a spirited young woman, while barely out of the schoolroom, to form a heady first attachment with a man who does not return her regard. The disappointed hopes she experiences when this gentleman turns his attentions elsewhere are among the bitterest a woman can feel. It is wise in such cases for the husband hunter to seek a change of situation. To remain among the scenes where the attachment was formed or among the company who saw it develop is to keep it alive in the memory in a way that is an obstacle to future happiness.

—The Husband Hunter's Guide to London

Chapter 2

"Harry, are you going to take the dog out?" Priscilla Luxborough huffed a little from the effort of climbing the stairs to Harriet's attic room. "I've been looking for you everywhere."

Harriet Swanley looked up from her book at her young cousin. "Oh, is it time?"

Pris shrugged, digging her hands in her pockets. "Are you reading anything good?"

Harriet closed her book and put it aside. "Emilie du Chatelet's *Discourses on Happiness.*"

Pris sighed. "Everyone's so dull today."

"That," said Harriet, "is on account of the gale last night." She knew Pris had missed her morning ride, as all of the Luxborough grooms were busy repairing damage to the stables from a fallen chimney.

Pris produced a card from the pocket she'd been digging in. "Oh, and you have a visitor."

As a governess, Harriet was not in the habit of receiving callers in Luxborough House. She couldn't keep the surprise from her voice. "Who's calling on me?"

"Here's his card." Pris offered a cream square of paper from her pocket. "I put him in the yellow room."

Harriet read the bold black lettering. *Charles Davenham, Viscount Wynford.* She jumped up, throwing off the burgundy shawl she'd wrapped around her shoulders for warmth. A night of wind blowing across the park and up Mount Street had cooled the house below the usual late November chill. "Pris, you didn't put a viscount in the yellow room. He's not a tradesman."

Again, Pris shrugged. "He's calling on *you*, not on the family. It must be about some business or other, and mother says business must always be conducted—"

"I know what your mother says, but viscounts do not belong in dingy backrooms. Did you send a footman to light a fire?"

Pris shook her head.

Harriet headed for the stairs. With any luck she'd reach Wynford before he froze solid.

Pris called after her, "Maybe the breakfast room is empty."

Maybe, Harriet thought, *I can become a paid governess in a house where my charges listen to me.* Harriet was under no illusion about her position in the Luxborough household, and, on the whole, it suited her. Her cousins had offered refuge when her family cast her off. In return she had shepherded a younger generation of Luxboroughs through their awkward years. They were a fine family of five. Ned, the eldest, was twenty-one. Anne, twenty, Camille, eighteen, and Pris, thirteen, were the middle children, and Jasper, at eleven was the last of Harriet's charges. The children, favored with their parents' fair good looks and happy manners, made the fate of tending them far superior to the one her brother had wished on her. When her circumstances chafed, as they sometimes did, she reminded herself that no one owned her body and soul, that she was free to think her own thoughts.

She opened the door to the yellow room, and a deeper cold hit her. She should not have left her shawl behind.

Viscount Lord Wynford knelt at the hearth, nursing a flame to life in a small pile of coals by the judicious application of a worn bellows as if he'd never depended on a servant in his life.

"I beg your pardon, Lord Wynford. Priscilla did not perfectly understand the protocol of receiving a gentleman of your..."

"...rank?" He rose to his full height, an amused glint in his hazel eyes. "Apparently, she considered your position rather than mine in directing me here." He left it at that.

Harriet had never supposed him to be dim. A mortifying burn flared in her cheeks. She willed it away. It had been ten years since she'd embarrassed herself in his presence. He would not remember that winter's day, and at six-and-twenty she would not disgrace herself again.

Those ten years had been kind to him. Manliness, she reflected, sneaking another glance at him as he put aside the bellows, was a hardier bloom than the mere prettiness of girls. At thirty-one, he was every bit as tall and solid and male as she remembered, his looks distilled by time to a lean, confident presence. He filled the small chamber and made its furnishings appear distinctly shabby.

"Would you prefer the morning room?" she asked. There she could put a table between them. "It is unoccupied at present."

"No, thank you." He glanced around. "A private room...suits my purpose. You see, I've come to ask a favor of you."

She was aware she was gaping. He could hardly have said anything more surprising. "Of me?"

"We are cousins, are we not?" He moved a plain wooden chair close to the hearth, holding it and looking at her. "Unless you are in training for a polar expedition, I recommend a seat near the fire."

His unexpected courtesy stirred wings of agitation in the pit of her stomach. They were cousins, she supposed, if one looked up the family tree for some great-great-great-grandfather in a periwig and silver-buckled heels. She gathered her wits and took the offered seat.

"Lady Harriet," he began. He pulled the other chair close and sat, studying her face briefly, then turned to look at the weak fire. "I will put this plainly. My younger sister Octavia has unexpectedly joined me in London. She wishes...to find a husband, and I have no experience with such an enterprise."

Harriet lowered her gaze to her lap. If she needed proof that he did not remember her, she had it, like a sharp jab in the ribs that momentarily stole her breath. A man who remembered the awkward, forward girl she'd been at sixteen wouldn't ask this favor. Men knew nothing of husband hunting. They were the hunted, after all, not the hunters. "What made you think of me?"

"You may not know it, but you have a friend and admirer in Peregrine Pilkington. Perry assures me you are a woman of great steadiness and sense." He spoke easily now that he had broken that first reserve. "Just the model Octavia needs."

"She has no governess or companion?"

"A country woman has been her nurse ever since...but Alice knows nothing of London society."

"Tell me a little more about your sister," Harriet invited. The girl must be an orphan. The previous viscount had died shortly after Napoleon's defeat at Waterloo, and his wife, years earlier, but Harriet could not remember what family history said about the late viscountess.

As Wynford spoke, she tried to concentrate on the flaws in his appearance. His face was too long, really. The brows above the deep-set hazel eyes were thick and dark as his hair, which fell from a rakish natural part over his left eye. Flaws and all, he remained handsome enough to flutter hearts more hardened than hers. She was, after all, apparently a woman of steadiness and sense, not one to arouse a handsome gentleman's admiration or feel unsettled in his presence.

At a pause in his explanation of his sister's longtime attachment to a neighboring squire's son, she said, "You do wish her to marry, don't you? It is expected of women."

"Not by Christmas, which is what she says she must do."

"Christmas! Oh my." Harriet wondered what had changed for the girl. Wynford's description suggested that Octavia had been living an uneventful country life with the expectation of marrying a near neighbor. It was not the desperate stuff of novels or high drama. "Do you know what precipitated this urgency?"

"She hasn't confided in me. I have encouraged her to stay in London for a proper Season in the spring."

"And?" He was holding something back. No doubt the reserve that had kept him from speaking easily at first still made it awkward for him to discuss his sister's situation with a relative stranger.

"She's got a book. *The Husband Hunter's Guide to London*. Have you read it?"

"I haven't." Harriet could not help smiling a little and raising a brow at the title. Poor Emilie du Chatelet had written about the foundations of physics and translated the great Newton into French, when perhaps, if she'd written about finding a husband, she'd have had thousands of readers.

"Octavia claims that, having read the book, she doesn't need any help to find a husband."

"What makes you think she'll accept my guidance then?"

"She's always been..."

"Biddable?" Harriet could not help the sudden grim set of her mouth.

He cast her a sharp glance. "I'm her brother. I've protected her since she was a babe. She's never..."

"Crossed you or flouted you? She's always needed you and depended on you?" Harriet's stomach knotted. She could listen no more. He was a man and an older brother. He believed it was his prerogative to decide how his sister was to be happy. Without knowing his sister's mind, he expected to be obeyed, as Harriet's brother Lionel had expected her to obey him and marry the man he chose, even if that man was a monster. She stood and crossed to the door before habits of politeness stopped her. She drew a breath and looked back. He had come to his feet, as trapped in politeness as she. "Forgive me," she said, turning to face him squarely. "I will be unable to help you."

A single coal crumbled in the grate.

"I beg your pardon. I've distressed or offended you," he said. His gaze did not waver. "Please tell me how and let me begin again."

Harriet took a shaky breath. She had only to dismiss him, and the interview would end. A scratching and whimpering at the door interrupted the thought. "Excuse me," she said. "I must see to the dog."

Again, Lord Wynford did not move. Harriet could see that he would not be dismissed easily. From the other side of the door the scratching and whimpering turned to a deep howl, a long echoing note followed by three shorter cries.

"I must go," she told her unmoving guest.

* * * *

The door closed behind her. The howling ceased. Charles heard her speak to the dog in a firm and friendly tone, and then the click of the beast's nails on the tiles as it followed her off.

He remained standing by the weak fire in the frigid room. Perry's description of Harriet Swanley as the steady unpaid governess to a large and careless family had misled him into thinking she would be the sort of woman no one noticed. He knew he had been introduced to a governess or two among the families of his acquaintance, and he supposed that he'd met such women with civility, but none had made an impression on him.

Lady Harriet Swanley did not fit the category. Instead of the neat and unassuming figure Perry's words had conjured, Charles had looked up from the cold hearth in the bare room and seen a softly beautiful countenance enlivened by eyes full of barely contained spirit. If he had been pressed to say what struck him about her, he would have to say it was a sense of controlled passion. The coil of her hair at her nape and the unadorned simplicity of her gown did not wholly conceal the riches of her appearance. Her brow was clear and her cheeks smooth as silk with a curve that invited a man's thumb to stroke. In her gray eyes he caught a silver glint of wit and a sense of the ridiculous.

He was grateful for the interruption provided by the dog. He could recover his wits and determine how to try again.

The door opened, and she stepped inside, her hand on the knob as if she would leave again. "I beg your pardon for the interruption."

"You're the dog-minder, too?" he asked. It spoke volumes about her state of absolute dependence on her relations that such tasks fell to her lot.

She laughed. "I suppose I am until Jasper returns from school. But you must not think the dog an imposition."

She gathered herself. He anticipated another refusal, but he cut her off. "Don't let me drive you from the fire, Lady Harriet," he said, extending a hand. "If you stand by the door, you'll turn into a block of ice."

After a brief hesitation, she accepted his hand and let herself be led back to a seat. "You mustn't judge my circumstances by this room. The Luxboroughs are kind, and..."

"Value you just as they ought?" He knew more about her situation than he would admit after a brief interview with Lady Luxborough, who had given him a rather shrewd look but had raised no objection to his request to enlist her governess's aid.

"I want for nothing," she said.

"Except, perhaps, independence? I know I'm speaking frankly, but I do need your help if Octavia is not to have her heart broken, or worse."

"What do you know of broken hearts, Lord Wynford?" Her eyes flashed.

"Nothing," he admitted.

Her gaze dropped to his boots, which she regarded with apparent fascination. He suspected she did not often look away. If self-control was the key to survival in London, she would be the very one to help Octavia.

"I will help your sister. Let us say that we are renewing our cousinly ties. But you must call me Miss Swanley, you know," she said briskly. "I have given up being called Lady Harriet."

He nodded.

She drew in a breath. "I know just the place where your sister can become accustomed to appearing in London society without feeling herself to be on display. Can you bring her to the Royal Institution on Monday afternoon?"

"The Royal Institution?"

"Yes. It's where Perry and I have met. The Christmas lectures begin Monday."

"Thank you," he said. "Octavia will enjoy that. She has a scientific bent."

She laughed. "Wait until Christmas to thank me, I think. Let me show you out, Lord Wynford."

At the door, he turned to the young footman, waiting with his hat, gloves, and coat, but before he could take them, a black-and-tan hound with a lean body and long, floppy ears barreled past them, his paws slipping on the marble. He lowered his hindquarters to the floor, sliding toward the open door. At the threshold he came to his feet again and launched himself through the door and down the steps. Evading a passing carriage, he bounded across the street to nose a pile of leaves and branches against the railings opposite.

"Excuse me, Lord Wynford," Miss Swanley said. "Duty calls. Timothy, can you get Cat's lead?"

Charles watched the dog push his nose deeper into the leaves. "His name is 'Cat'?"

"For Catapult. He bolts when he sees daylight."

"Ah. Will he come to a stranger?"

"He might, but don't let me keep you."

Charles ignored the dismissal. Apparently Miss Harriet Swanley was a woman who did not readily seek help. He crossed the street to the pile of storm debris where the dog still nosed about, picked up a stout stick, and called the dog's name.

Cat lifted his head, turning toward the voice of authority. Charles waited until the stick caught and held the dog's gaze. Then he tossed it in Miss Swanley's direction. It landed a few feet in front of her. Cat bounded after it, pounced, and began to crunch the stick happily. Miss Swanley slipped a lead around his neck.

Charles strolled back her way, conscious of the cold November gusts ruffling his hair. "What is he?" he asked. Cat now sat at Miss Swanley's feet, a picture of canine obedience.

"He's an unfortunate mix of French and English foxhound."

"Why unfortunate?" He extended a hand to stroke the dog's head.

"He absolutely refuses to hunt." She grinned at him. "Do not pet him, by the way. He will not forget you and will insist on receiving such attentions ever after."

Charles regarded her narrowly. Something teased his memory. "Have we met before?"

"I am sure I would remember if we had," she told him, sobering at once and looking at a point over his left shoulder.

*There is genuine pleasure in being noticed. However, the
husband hunter does not want to purchase the inferior goods of
being a mere distraction, of catching a man's eye because of the
feathers in her bonnet. Rather, she wants the true gratification
of being recognized, of having a gentleman direct his eyes and
indeed his footsteps her way, not because she has caught his eye
with her plumage but because he seeks her company.*

—The Husband Hunter's Guide to London

Chapter 3

Harriet was spared a second encounter with Lord Wynford when his
friend Perry brought Octavia to the Royal Institution the following Monday.
With his interest in science, Perry was a regular attendee at the institution's
lectures and gatherings. His easy manners made him one of the few people
from the world she'd left behind that she met with pleasure.

Since meeting Wynford and agreeing to help his sister, Harriet had thought
better of her answer to his final question. Something in their conversation
had stirred his memory, and she feared he might recall later how and where
they'd met. She had not lied when she said she would remember a previous
meeting between them, but she would, perhaps, have been wiser to suggest
that they *had* met in some wholly unremarkable way in London.

In the foyer of the Royal Institution, Perry introduced Miss Davenham,
giving an uncharacteristically muddled explanation for accompanying her
in Wynford's stead. Obviously, Wynford was occupied in the gentlemanly
pursuits of a man of rank and means. Harriet performed her part by
introducing the two eldest Luxborough girls, Anne and Camille, who
welcomed Octavia warmly.

There was a strong resemblance between the sister and brother except
in the stricken look in Octavia's light brown eyes and the limpness of her
posture, which suggested a fever victim rather than a girl eager to take on
London.

Harriet knew what it was to live inside that lost look and what it took to
overcome it, and she was glad to see the girl rally, opening the strings of her
reticule and drawing out a small blue volume with gold filigree lettering.
Harriet glanced at the title—*The Husband Hunter's Guide to London.*

"Cousin," Octavia said, clutching the little book to her chest. "Charles tells me I must depend on you to set me on the path to a husband by Christmas, but I promise not to trouble you much. I have my book, you see."

Harriet applauded Octavia's instinct to be active but doubted that husband hunting would mend a broken heart. A suitor or two tossing lavish compliments her way might offer a balm to wounded pride, but something more was needed for true healing.

Harriet had been fortunate in her time of anguish to be given a consuming task and to find in that task a part of herself, both generous and strong-minded, she had not known she possessed. It had given her great confidence. She would have to think of some occupation that might suit Octavia as well. If the girl truly had a scientific bent, there would be something.

Around them, people poured into the institution with the usual buzz of gathering and greeting. Anne and Camille noted several young gentlemen and exchanged nods with friends. There was a momentary hush as Mr. Faraday himself passed through the crowd. He had instituted the lectures the year before.

"Must speak with Faraday," Perry announced. With a brief bow, he hurried off.

"Faraday!" Octavia pivoted to look after him, then sighed and turned back to Harriet. "He's a fine scientist, but not an eligible gentleman, is he?"

"No," Harriet said gently. It was a little slip on the girl's part, a brief show of excitement over seeing the great scientist, quickly quelled by whatever troubled the girl and made her clutch the little book like a lifeline. "He's the director at the moment, and of course, the founder, just last year, of these lectures."

"Of course," said Octavia, tucking her book away. "But it's eligible gentlemen I must seek. I've no time to waste, you see."

The look in Octavia's eye struck Harriet as grim determination. The girl had seized on the idea of hunting a husband as a rider on a runaway horse might mistakenly tighten her arms on the reins and lock her back, measures that only made it easier for the horse to throw her.

"Come along," Harriet said to the three girls. They passed into the round lecture hall with its high ceilings, tall yellow columns, and ascending half-circle of seats and found a place on the cushioned benches about halfway up the chamber, looking down on a table set with glass and metal tubes, stoppered vials, and candles. Harriet loved the drama of the scene. The speaker would set before them some common mystery of the world in all its puzzling detail and unveil the scientific principles behind the seeming magic.

Once seated, Octavia retrieved the book from her reticule and held it in her lap, nodding politely as Anne and Camille pointed out the features of the room and named people around them.

"There are children here," Octavia said to Harriet during a break in the other conversation, the statement more accusation than observation.

There were children, especially on the packed lower benches directly in front of the speaker's table and instruments. It was Mr. Faraday's intention to make science exciting to the young. "Yes," she said, "but you may ignore them and concentrate on the eligible gentlemen if you like."

"I must, mustn't I?" Octavia said with sudden resolve. "Won't they all be dreadfully old, like Charles?"

Harriet suppressed a laugh. "What do you consider the ideal age for a husband?"

"My book says... " Octavia idly turned the pages of the volume in her lap. "Well, I don't remember precisely what the book says, but I think three and twenty the right age."

"No older?"

"Not at all, for a man must be independent of his parents and must have some experience in managing his affairs, but he must not be hardened."

"And a man of twenty-four is, in your opinion, hardened?"

"Terribly."

Harriet resisted the impulse to give the girl's hands a quick squeeze, as she would for Anne or Camille. She did not yet understand Octavia's situation though she strongly suspected some recent heartache. There had been a time when Harriet, too, had thought four and twenty a most advanced age. She guessed that a young man wielding his wider experience of the world had wounded Octavia. From the way the girl clung to her book, Harriet suspected the wound was both deep and new.

A distraction at the entrance drew all eyes. A group of young men, Ned Luxborough among them, entered the hall, talking and laughing and exchanging playful whacks with their hats. Octavia sat up straight and put on a bright smile. One young man looked up and waved at Anne and Camille before he and his companions swarmed up the aisle and clambered over several benches into the upper reaches of the seats, passing Octavia without a glance her way.

Only one of them paused at the entrance to their row to apologize for his friends. He was a sturdy young man with a sweep of golden hair, ruddy cheeks, and deep blue eyes, soberly—almost clerically—dressed in charcoal gray. "Miss Swanley, isn't it?" he asked Harriet.

She nodded.

"Thought so," he said, his gaze on Octavia. "John Jowers, friend of Ned Luxborough from school. We're all Wykehamists, you know." He shrugged, as if the school affiliation explained their behavior, and cleared his throat. "Could you present me to your friend, Miss Swanley?"

Harriet nodded again, and made the introduction.

Octavia offered an artificial smile.

"Are you keen on science, Miss Davenham?" Mr. Jowers asked.

For a moment Harriet thought Octavia would acknowledge an interest, but some struggle seemed to occur. She clutched her reticule and, with an affected air of boredom, said, "Not really."

"Oh," he said. "You might change your mind, you know."

He bowed and retreated up the benches.

A moment later Octavia lamented, "No one even looks at me."

"Mr. Jowers looked at you," Harriet said, offering a mild correction. She could hear the pain in the girl's voice, a pain that no doubt made it impossible for Octavia to see clearly.

"I will have to change my appearance." Octavia turned the pages of her book again.

"Shall we plan a shopping expedition?" Harriet asked.

"Oh yes," said Octavia, "it says right here that 'the husband hunter must be seen, and therefore, must take great care of her appearance.'"

The clock struck the hour, and the lecture began. It was possibly the least attention Harriet had given to a lecture in a long time. Next to her, Octavia alternately slumped or straightened, occasionally letting the lecture capture her interest then retreating into her stance of bored indifference.

"What sort of cousin are you, Miss Swanley?" she asked at one point.

"A fourth cousin," Harriet whispered. "We share a great-great-great-grandfather."

At the end of the lecture, Ned Luxborough led the young gentlemen to join Anne and Camille in a laughing group, except for John Jowers. He stopped as Octavia and Harriet prepared to exit their row.

"Brilliant lecture, Miss Davenham. Did you like it?" he asked.

Octavia, her head held unnaturally high, said, "Hardly."

"Well, perhaps you'll like the next one better." Mr. Jowers bowed and joined his friends.

"The next one?" Octavia looked at Harriet.

"There will be six," Harriet said firmly. "All attended by young gentlemen."

"Oh." Octavia straightened her shoulders. "Then I must attend."

"Perhaps you would prefer dancing. If your brother can spare you, would you like to join the Luxboroughs at a gathering tonight?"

"Dancing? Oh yes." The girl cast a wistful glance at Anne and Camille and their friends.

"The guests will be closer in age to your ideal than your brother's friends."

"It's sad, isn't it?" Octavia said, as they descended the stairs. "I suppose Charles was quite handsome in his day."

"His day?"

"When he was one and twenty and came into his title, I think there were ladies then who wanted to marry him. But now that he's one and thirty, I don't suppose he will ever marry."

Harriet choked back a laugh. Octavia's notion that her brother, surely one of the most eligible bachelors in London, had entered his dotage explained a lot. The girl was unlikely to confide in a brother she regarded as past hope of marrying.

They reached the street, and Harriet was beginning to wonder where Perry had got to and how she was to convey her guest home when Octavia said, "Look, there's Charles."

Harriet followed Octavia's gaze down Albemarle Street to a building she rarely considered. It was near enough to the Royal Institution that she'd passed it often. She had hardly given it much thought other than to sympathize with whoever was wishing for its completion. It was a neighborhood eyesore in a perpetual state of renovation with scaffolding and flapping canvas sheets across a portico that jutted out into the walkway. She just caught sight of Wynford as he ducked under the canvas.

Then Perry was there. "Sorry to desert you so long," he said. With his perpetually youthful face he had the look of a guilty schoolboy. "Needed Faraday's help."

"Perry," said Octavia. "What is Charles doing in that derelict old building?"

Perry glanced at the building Octavia indicated and shrugged his shoulders. "It's some sort of club or other. I believe your brother is one of the...investors, trying to get the place going. How was the lecture?"

Harriet thought Wynford an unlikely investor in a club, but Perry had turned Octavia's thoughts. She answered with a surprising grasp of what they had heard and talked unaffectedly to Perry while they waited for their carriage. Harriet took note of the girl's natural, unconstrained manner with an old friend whom she did not regard as a potential husband, so different from her stilted conversation with John Jowers.

* * * *

The Marchioness de Tonnelier was not a woman to be overlooked in a crowd. The particular crowd in which Charles found her had assembled in the Duchess of Huntington's long gallery for the unveiling of a new painting the duke had acquired.

More handsome than beautiful, with smoky dark eyes, red lips, and no attempt to disguise those imperfections of hair and face that mark a sexually confident woman, the marchioness had a distinctly French air about her. Nothing was wrong with her figure in a gown of rich ruby silk that bared her white shoulders. The one unanticipated aspect of her appearance was her size. The top of her head below the black plumes of her satin toque just reached the stickpin in his cravat. The contrast between the childlike body and cynical face was striking. Charles guessed her to be a few years older than his own thirty-one years.

Apparently, a spy did not need to blend in or seek the shadows. The boldness of her appearance, much as it repelled Charles, seemed calculated to draw men to her side. At such a gathering, many of the available men had ties to the government. He watched to see which man appeared to be her target.

As he stood contemplating his opening move in the game to unmask her, Perry strolled his way, a glass of wine in hand.

"Hello, you look..." Perry glanced at Charles's striped green-and-gold waistcoat. "Vivid."

"If I fail to expose the marchioness, I think I should ask Astley for a job in his circus."

Perry nodded. "Should do the trick then. The marchioness will never suspect you of deep intellectual powers."

"If she's willing to talk to me at all in this getup. Did you find out anything more about her connections to my family?"

Perry shook his head. "Faraday suggested a chemical test of the paper and ink to see how old they are."

Charles nodded. He kept an eye on the marchioness in conversation with two gentlemen—one of them, Edenhorn, a singularly dull MP with a post at the Exchequer and endless knowledge of the recent bullion crisis.

The duke's footmen passed among the crowd, filling glasses, while the duke and duchess made their way to a small dais next to the painting, concealed behind a red velvet curtain. Charles stepped forward, until he stood at the marchioness's elbow.

Someone tapped a glass, and the talk died down as all turned to the duke.

"As many of you know, England lost a great treasure some years ago when Walpole sold his collection to the Russians. At the time, I and others proposed in Parliament the establishment of a national gallery." The stately, white-haired duke paused. He was known for the quizzing glass dangling from a pale blue ribbon around his neck as well as his withering condescension. "However, it was not to be, and until the nation demands such an institution, the people of England must rely on the private collector to preserve its treasures. My dear?" He turned to the duchess, who pulled a golden cord.

The velvet curtains parted on a painting by the French artist Poussin, a striking image of an angel descending to address a maiden in a vivid blue robe.

Charles watched the marchioness. She did not show the least sign of recognition of the painting, though Charles knew it had once hung in the Musee Napoleon in Paris, where most Parisians could have seen it.

He turned to his companion.

"It is a great shame, is it not," he observed, "when nations cannot keep their own art."

His comment drew a dry smile and an amused glance from the marchioness. "Have we met, *monsieur*?" she asked.

"I am Wynford," he said. "Are we not family?"

Her expression changed. A quick calculation passed in her eyes. Whatever she had heard of him, she had not expected the vulgar excess of his waistcoat. "Ah, you are my cousin, are you not? The son of Charlotte."

She knew his pedigree, and he heard no obvious flaws in her accent, which sounded pure Parisian.

"What draws you to London when you could be in Paris?" he asked.

"Alas, I must look after some documents my late father-in-law sent to your country for safekeeping. It is tedious but necessary to establish one's claims to lost property in France."

"Which of Delatour lands do you hope to recover?" Charles thought it a mild challenge, a test to see whether she remembered those vineyards.

She did not blink. "The Saumur vineyards. Saumur was not so revolutionary-minded a place as some. Its people are practical where there is a profit to be made, and I hope the property will soon be restored to the Delatours." She took a sip of wine.

"Ah," he said, trying to check his suspicions and keep his head clear.

Her bare shoulders rose and fell in a quintessentially Gallic shrug. "Do you know the Saumur vineyards?"

"Only from summers as a boy." He had been in Saumur for the harvest during a brief peace before the fatal trip with his mother and Octavia. He remembered a steep cobbled street of gabled houses below a great castle, grapes in deep purple clusters, and the sure rapidity of the pickers with their straw hats and gloved hands and small, curved knives.

"It is not perhaps the best time to be in London, as my new friends tell me that the town empties soon for you English to have your Christmas in the country. It is the custom, is it not? Are you not obliged to go home to your own lands to be with your sister?"

It was an easy lie and quite credible except for the mention of his sister. Octavia was unknown in London to all but Charles's closest friends, like Perry, and Perry had not been talking to the marchioness. "Ah," he said, "I'm an idle town fellow, and rarely feel obliged to do anything." He swirled the wine in his glass. "Which of your vintages would you recommend?"

Before she could answer, there was a little stir in the room as Wellington entered and the crowd parted, everyone following his progress to the duke and duchess's side. Ten years after Wellington's defeat of Napoleon, eager hostesses considered his appearance at a gathering a social triumph. When the great man neared Charles and the marchioness, she turned away abruptly, extending her empty wine glass to a passing footman.

No one noticed except Charles. It was a small thing, perhaps unintended, meant to look spontaneous and flustered, but Charles doubted the marchioness ever gave way to impulse.

"Have you been introduced to our national hero?" Charles asked.

"Oh one meets him everywhere," she said, turning back to Charles with an abstracted air, her face still averted from Wellington's gaze. "What were we speaking of before?" She moved her fan gently in front of her face.

"It was nothing," he said. "Perhaps another time you will tell me more about your wine."

"Let it be soon." She smiled a dismissive smile. "Pardon me."

He bowed and stepped aside. He watched her stroll down the long gallery, unhurried, pausing to look at the art and speak with other guests. He could not say who had won this first skirmish. He had perhaps betrayed a weakness in his response to the mention of his sister. He had observed no flaw in the woman's disguise, if it was a disguise, except perhaps her strange reaction to Wellington. The great duke, a notorious flirt, was known to be susceptible to handsome women, and of all the gentlemen in London, he possessed the influence to help a woman in need of recovering property in France. How interesting that the marchioness chose to avoid rather than seek the great duke.

* * * *

From a chair against the wall, Harriet watched as the full disaster of Octavia's first London evening unfolded. Lady Luxborough, an accommodating parent, had arranged for the rugs in her drawing room to be rolled up and provided a piano player and a dancing master to instruct her children in preparation for a Twelfth Night ball when the family returned from the country.

Octavia had not consulted Harriet about what to wear, and the girl's choice, a high-waisted gown of pale pink aflutter with rose-colored ribbons, looked distinctly out of place among the shining dark silks and lush velvets the other young ladies wore.

Octavia alternately beamed and scowled. There were enough guests, young friends of the Luxboroughs, to make seven couples, and every gentleman asked Octavia to dance once, but no gentleman looked at her again after fulfilling the obligation of politeness. At a break in the dancing only Mr. John Jowers, their acquaintance from the Royal Institution lecture, approached Octavia. He came bearing a cup of steaming punch.

Standing next to Harriet's chair, Octavia appeared not to see him, her gaze focused on a lively group around Anne and Camille Luxborough. "They're all just being polite, aren't they?" she observed to no one in particular.

Mr. Jowers held out the cup for Octavia. "That's because you bounce too much."

"What?" she asked sharply, no longer ignoring him.

"You bounce, you know. The other girls glide. A fellow doesn't like to get..." His glance dropped to the cup in his hand. "So distracted."

Octavia frowned darkly. "And are you such a great dancer, Mr. Jowers?"

"At least I know the difference between a country reel and the quadrille."

"Well you needn't dance with me again if you don't like my dancing."

Octavia walked off leaving him holding the cup of punch, its little curl of steam dissipating in the air while he looked for some way to rid himself of the evidence of his dismissal.

Harriet said, "I'll take the punch if you like, Mr. Jowers."

"Yes," he said. "Thank you." He handed the cup to Harriet and turned back to stare at the others. "Someone has to tell her, you know. She doesn't know how to get on in London."

"Yes," Harriet agreed.

"And she wants partners, doesn't she?"

"Very much." Harriet understood his confusion. Whatever hurt had driven Octavia to London was making her blind to John Jowers's notice.

"I didn't say anything about her dress. She looks like a Maypole in that gown."

"Very wrong for this occasion."

"So..." He turned to Harriet directly. "Why wouldn't she listen to friendly advice?" In his voice Harriet heard the baffled lament of a young man newly come from school, where one was rewarded for being right without the necessity of being tactful as well.

"Ah," said Harriet. "She is, as you say, new to London, and feeling unsure of herself. She may not be ready to hear her errors proclaimed so directly."

He made no reply. The musician returned to his instrument, and the dancing master summoned his pupils. Mr. Jowers sighed. "Will you take her to another of the Royal Institution lectures?"

"I will," Harriet assured him. He bowed and returned to the crowd of young people arranging themselves in two lines for another set.

Harriet smiled to herself. If John Jowers meant to pursue his interest in Octavia, there was time for the girl to recover from whatever misery made her unseeing at present. She might be weeping, or more likely, gritting her teeth and resolving to gain the notice of her new friends by some reformation of her appearance, but she had made a conquest. One she might despise, but one that would do her no harm and might even steer her toward more comfort in London society.

John Jowers's directness had no doubt pricked the girl's pride, but Jowers saw only the easily corrected flaws. His words would prompt Octavia to change her dress and her steps. The bigger project, as Harriet saw it, belonged to her, to help the girl think of others rather than only of herself. Someone had made her feel flawed, and she had lost the confidence to be her natural self.

Harriet rose to go in search of her charge and came face to face with Wynford. He wore a striped green-and-gold waistcoat that halted her in her tracks.

He bowed, surveying the room with a searching gaze. "Where's Octavia?" he asked, the sharpness of his tone at odds with the pleasant scene of innocent enjoyment.

"Hello," she said. "I'll fetch her. She needed a moment to collect herself."

"She's quite safe?" he asked.

Harriet frowned, puzzled by his anxiety, which seemed out of place in such comfortable domestic surroundings. "In Lady Luxborough's drawing room? It is only that Octavia made some mistakes such as young ladies are apt to make their first time in company."

"You didn't stop her?"

"I didn't. She must be permitted to make a few missteps if she is to learn how to get on in London."

He glanced at the dancers, and she let him take in their utterly harmless appearance.

"Has Octavia had a recent disappointment in love?" she asked.

"In love?" He turned back to Harriet with a baffled look.

"Yes, you know," she said, endeavoring to lift her gaze from the eye-popping waistcoat, "that state of mind in which people fancy themselves deeply attached to another."

"Octavia's never fancied herself in love. She and our neighbor Horace Gresham have been intended for one another since childhood."

He spoke as if he'd never questioned the prospect. "By whom? Their parents? You?"

"No, entirely by their own inclinations. They've been inseparable companions since they rode their first ponies together."

"Really? How old is this neighbor now?"

"Four and twenty, I think. Does it matter?"

Harriet thought it mattered a great deal. "Don't you find it odd that your sister should come to London declaring her intention of finding a husband by Christmas if she already has a fixed attachment?"

It was a moment before he answered. She sensed that he was thinking for the first time about the suddenness of Octavia's desire for a husband. A waltz tune appeared to catch his attention. "You must think me quite oblivious."

"Distracted, perhaps."

"Charitable of you to put it that way," he said stiffly. "Has she confided in you?"

Harriet shook her head. She knew the patience required to win a young person's confidence. Until Octavia did confide in someone, there was no way of knowing whether something had changed between her and Horace Gresham, or whether her brother had misread their relationship all along. "You did say she had an interest in science?"

"Astronomy, actually. She's a habitual stargazer and quite a fanatic about the moon. She's been recording her observations of the moon in her sketchbook for years."

Harriet nodded, more certain than ever that Octavia had suffered a loss of affection that made her wish to reject every aspect of her true self in favor of affecting the airs of a fashionable London miss. "Let me find her. She may need the comfort of your presence."

As the husband hunter establishes herself in a circle of acquaintance in London, she may not at first observe any disparities of fortune among the gentlemen who solicit her hand for a dance or vie to bring her into supper. A nobody from nowhere, heir to nothing, may be as charming, well-spoken, and fashionable as the next man, as sought after by hostesses to make up their numbers. But the husband hunter must beware, the more attractive this nobody, the graver the danger he poses to her happiness. He is as unacceptable to her family as an islander living in a hut next door to Robinson Crusoe. Whether the family is of long standing in the peerage or newly risen into the realm of gentility, it is the chief concern of her parents to secure their daughter's station in life.

—The Husband Hunter's Guide to London

Chapter 4

The following afternoon, Lord Wynford himself accompanied Octavia and Harriet and the Luxborough party to the Royal Institution. Whether the brother and sister had spoken of Octavia's situation or not, Harriet suspected that Wynford meant to observe his sister more closely. He might be excessively protective, but Harriet could not accuse him of being indifferent to Octavia's happiness.

They arrived in good time and made their way through the lobby and into the theater. Lord Wynford had returned to his usual understated elegance, and Octavia wore a becoming gown of pale blue wool that set off her fair complexion and dark hair. But she refused to look at or speak to her brother.

When they reached the row of seats Harriet preferred, Octavia went ahead with her new friends, so as to avoid sitting next to her brother. Wynford appeared not to notice, reserving his civility for Harriet. It was the merest politeness, but a novel sensation flustered her briefly at being the object of a gentleman's attentions. She had for so long followed her charges in and out of rooms, she had forgotten any other arrangement.

"I'm in disgrace," Wynford confided to Harriet.

"What have you done?" she asked. She expected him to confess that he had pressed Octavia to confide in him, and that the girl had refused.

"I suggested the blue gown."

"Suggested?" Harriet challenged him. "Admit it, you would not permit her to leave the house in..."

"A striped sarcenet better suited to a country picnic or a shop awning."

Harriet did not understand him. It was an odd remark from a man who had worn stripes the night before. And they plainly disagreed on how to guide a young woman to sound judgment.

Their conversation was interrupted by an exchange of greetings with some of Lady Luxborough's acquaintances. Necessary introductions were made, and Harriet read in the other ladies' faces their astonishment at her companion's name and rank.

"Are you embarrassed to be seen with me, Miss Swanley?" he asked as she scrupulously tucked away her reticule and gloves.

"Not at all."

"Then perhaps it is the heat of the room that brings that pink color into your cheeks."

"Am I so obvious?" she asked. "A governess, you know, is obliged to remain invisible. I'm afraid appearing with you, even in your sister's company, smacks of putting myself forward."

"Surely, your friends know you better," he suggested gently.

"It is Lady Luxborough's friends in whose eyes I have trespassed."

It was not quite a rebuke, but it checked him briefly, and before he offered a rejoinder, Perry came bounding up the aisle.

Perry gave Harriet the briefest of nods. Octavia still refused to look her brother's way.

"Quick, man," Perry said to Wynford. "The marchioness is here. I've brought a waistcoat. No time to lose." He waved a garment in a startling shade of purple.

"Pardon me," Wynford said to Harriet, and followed Perry to the upper reaches of the theater.

"Hah," Octavia said, turning to Harriet.

"I gather that you and your brother have had a falling-out."

"He makes no sense. One evening he can wear a waistcoat striped like a tiger, and the next day he tells me I can't go near stripes."

"Baffling, I agree," said Harriet. "What explains it, do you think?" She had not missed Perry's reference to a marchioness, though she could not imagine why a man of Wynford's usual restrained dress should don the peacock hues of the previous century for a woman.

"It's downright provoking if you ask me, Miss Swanley. If you don't have a brother, you can have mine."

There were still a few minutes before the hour, and Anne and Camille engaged Octavia in a discussion of the merits of the young gentlemen from the previous evening.

"There were some quite handsome," Octavia acknowledged, "and your brother Ned is the best dancer, far better than...anyone else." Octavia grew quiet. "I suppose he didn't ask me to dance again because... Oh well, I daresay, I will learn to dance in the London way."

"Oh no," Camille hastened to reassure her. "That's just Ned's way. He is scrupulously polite. He dances with each girl once."

As Octavia weighed this alternate interpretation of the evening, John Jowers appeared at the end of their row and bowed.

"You," said Octavia.

"I'm glad you came for another lecture, Miss Davenham. Today Wallis is going to talk about the movement of the planets."

"I thought astronomy was about stars," Octavia said with an obvious sense of grievance.

Mr. Jowers obliged the ladies to stand and shift their positions, and took a seat beside Octavia. "Stars are fine to look at," he said, "but it's the planets that explain everything."

"I really prefer stars," Octavia insisted. "Planets are what—lumps of dirt and rock?"

Undeterred by Octavia's apparent distaste for the topic, Mr. Jowers launched into an explanation of the Newtonian modification of Kepler's third law of motion. He was deep into mathematical details of mass and gravity and the semimajor axes of elliptical orbits when Lord Wynford, wearing the shocking purple waistcoat, slipped back into place beside Harriet.

He had no sooner seated himself than a woman entered the hall, drawing all eyes. There was no denying the elegance of her satin pelisse in a rich myrtle-green trimmed with fur. Her face was striking under the brim of a bronze silk bonnet, and her bold gaze went at once to Wynford.

Beside Harriet, Octavia gave a small start of surprise. "Oh," she said, "that's how one is supposed to dress."

The striking marchioness obviously had a sense of style, but it was just the sort to mislead the novice into fatal imitation. Before Harriet could correct Octavia's notion that the dress appropriate to a woman well past thirty should be her model, the woman reached them and stopped.

Wynford stood. "Marchioness."

"Cousin." She withdrew a gloved hand from a rich chinchilla muff and extended it to Wynford. "I did not know you had scientific interests." Her amused glance flickered over the outrageous waistcoat.

"Hardly," he said with curt civility. "I merely accompany my...sister and her...companion."

"Your sister," said the marchioness. "You must make us acquainted."

Wynford made the introductions with stiff correctness, relegating Harriet to the role of governess rather than relation without a blink. Harriet had not seen him so ill at ease and so little able to conceal it, his brusque manner at odds with his words. He did not wish his sister to become acquainted with the Frenchwoman.

"Ah, little cousin," said the marchioness to Octavia with a sly smile. "We shall become acquainted, *n'est-ce pas?* Your mother was my cousin, too."

"Marchioness, you will want your seat," said Wynford, "as the lecture begins promptly with the hour."

Harriet quietly abandoned the notion that she would learn much from Mr. Wallis's lecture. Gravity might be the universal law that governed everything, from apples or the coins in one's pocket to the planets in their orbits around the sun, but other laws governed the motion of hearts.

There are in London, besides the hundred or more churches built by men such as Wren, Gibbs, and Hawksmoor, certain secular temples of fashion to which the female worshipper of style is drawn. These commercial temples have their lofty ceilings, vast expanses, and high priests. And the husband hunter who wishes to step out of the common mold and assume a style of her own must repair to them nearly as often as she attends Sunday services at the Chapel Royal.

—*The Husband Hunter's Guide to London*

Chapter 5

An opportunity arose the following morning for Harriet to fulfill her promise of a shopping expedition. She was able to invite Octavia to Luxborough House, where Lady Luxborough and her two eldest daughters were making a serious study of the latest fashion plates in preparation for a visit to the linen drapers Harding Howell & Co. Each girl was to have a gown for the Luxboroughs' annual Twelfth Night Ball, marking the family's January return to London from their Hampshire estate.

For the most part Octavia was a silent onlooker, observing the frank sisterly exchange of Anne and Camille. The sisters did not hesitate to abuse each other's taste and shortcomings of face and figure. Camille told Anne that with her short neck she could not wear a much-admired teal blue velvet choker, while Anne, just as pointedly, told Camille that lace puff sleeves on a rose silk gown would not do for her plump arms. When Octavia sighed over a bold plaid, both sisters firmly turned the page. But when they came to the plate of a ball gown in lavender satin with a silver gauze overdress and tiny pearl-studded cap sleeves, both sisters turned to their guest.

"Octavia, this would look lovely on you," said Anne. "Neither Camille nor I could wear it, but on you it would be just right. What do you think, Harry? Do you think it would suit her?"

Harriet had to agree—and to feel a certain satisfaction that her lessons had not entirely gone awry. Her pupils were capable of taste and kindness, and their opinion appeared to sway Octavia from choosing a gown more appropriate to the bold Frenchwoman they had seen at the Royal Institution the day before.

"Do come with us to the shops," Camille begged. "I'm sure we can find you some of this lavender satin, and you can have your gown made up with ours in time for Twelfth Night."

With a little more conversation it was settled that Octavia would send a message to her brother about her shopping plans. Lady Luxborough gave her approval to the more modest of her daughters' dress choices, and with as much dispatch as five ladies could manage, they were off.

At the linen draper's, Octavia was taken with the great bolts of Turkish satin in lemon, lavender, and cerulean blue. She looked wistfully at a Pomona green striped *gros de Naples* before settling down in earnest to the purchase of the necessary yards of lavender satin and silver gauze. She flushed with pleasure as the clerk tallied her purchases at the counter.

"Of course," she told Harriet with a certain wistfulness, "I will have a husband by Twelfth Night, but even a married woman can be fashionable."

"What's this?" A husky voice made them turn. The marchioness, as strikingly elegant as the day before in a geranium-colored silk pelisse with a full chemisette of French cambric at the collar and her chinchilla muff, laid a gloved hand on Octavia's silk.

"How charming!" she said. "Just the sort of tender shade that becomes a young girl. Alas, one can never wear that pale look again after twenty. But are you so soon to marry, cousin?"

Octavia, looking awestruck, simply nodded.

Harriet tucked Octavia's arm in hers. "It is the way with our loveliest girls. They are soon claimed." It was irrational, she knew, but she, who was used to endless careless slights, disliked the superiority of the Frenchwoman's tone.

The marchioness smiled, and Harriet reined in the mad impulse to drag Octavia away. It was the most ordinary of London scenes. Nothing threatened. Harriet had no reason for the foolish alarm Wynford seemed to feel. Around them, ladies continued their chatter and their buying. Lady Luxborough stood not three feet away, engaged in arranging for her footmen to collect their purchases. Harriet supposed she simply had insufficient experience of French persons to judge the woman's behavior. She thought it coldly calculated to undermine Octavia's confidence in her fashion choice, but perhaps it was merely the woman's unfamiliarity with the rules that governed young English girls.

"But why the rush to marriage?" the marchioness asked. "Surely, cousin, you wish to know the world a little before you turn...matron."

If the marchioness thought to frighten Octavia with such an unfashionable word, she was mistaken. Octavia stuck out her chin. "Oh, I've quite made up my mind in the matter."

The marchioness shrugged. "How very English. Tell me, does your governess insist on Gowland's lotion for the complexion and a milk-and-water style gown for balls?"

"Oh, Miss Swanley is not—"

Harriet stopped Octavia with a squeeze of her arm. "Lady Luxborough wants us. Pray excuse us, Marchioness."

Nods were exchanged, and Harriet and Octavia moved toward the Luxborough party.

"Wasn't her hat marvelous?" Octavia whispered.

Harriet laughed. "It was," she agreed, her sense of grievance melting away. Admiration for the marchioness's good taste in bonnets was not likely to harm Octavia in any way.

* * * *

Hours later Harriet took a last look around Lady Luxborough's second-best drawing room, the customary gathering place for Harriet and her charges when the Luxboroughs were engaged elsewhere for the evening. A young footman named Timothy cleared away the evening tea things while Harriet collected the playing cards and various items the girls had left behind. Though the marchioness might wear marvelous hats, her interference earlier in the day still rankled. Harriet wondered at the woman's motive for disparaging English governesses. It was a small drop of malice in an otherwise satisfying day, and she tried to laugh at herself. The woman was no one to her, and perhaps national pride made the marchioness think French governesses superior to their English counterparts. Harriet doubted they were so very different.

Once she'd tidied up, she could retire to her room, read her book, and forget the marchioness. If anything, the day had proved the worth and value of her work. Anne and Camille had been thoughtful and generous to Octavia, and besides the ball gown, Octavia had been willing to purchase some Genoa velvet and kerseymere to be made up into warm dresses. Satisfied with the state of the room, Harriet turned to leave as the door opened.

Lady Luxborough's butler, Blakemore, announced, "Miss, you have a caller."

"At this hour?"

"Lord Wynford, miss. He asks you to meet him in the yellow room."

Harriet tried to remain calm as she descended the stairs. Only the lateness of the hour suggested any cause for alarm.

The little room was as cold as she remembered. Three candles in a silver stand on the mantel gave a weak yellow light. With her entry, Wynford turned from staring into the dark hearth. He was dressed for an evening engagement, everything about him easy and elegant except for a number of fobs and rings and another shocking waistcoat, this one of scarlet velvet.

London delighted in eccentrics, many of whom paraded their particular oddities at the fashionable hour in the park, but Harriet had never seen Wynford make a display of such quirks. She wondered if he'd traded waistcoats with one of the famous Bow Street Runners, but the gravity of his expression when he looked at her drove such levity from her mind.

"What is it?" she asked, stepping closer and drawing her burgundy India shawl around her to keep from reaching out to him.

"I need to know where you take my sister and with whom she is in company at all times."

Harriet stepped back abruptly as if slapped.

"You object to Lady Luxborough's drawing room and the linen draper's?"

"In future I wish you to send word of exactly where you mean to go and with—"

"We did, my lord. Your sister is very much in need of clothes more suited to London than those she brought with her."

The severity of his frown did not lessen, the dark brows drawn together, his posture rigid and haughty. "Nevertheless, the utmost care must be taken with her acquaintance."

"To whom in Lady Luxborough's circle could you possibly object?"

His expression hardened, and he turned his angry, tight-lipped countenance away.

Harriet recognized his cold manner from the day before at the Royal Institution. "Oh, this is about the marchioness," she said.

His gaze swung back to her, and he uttered one clipped syllable. "Yes."

"You cannot imagine I would willingly seek to bring Octavia into contact with a woman of such bold assurance. She may be your cousin, but in my considered opinion, as a governess," she said it proudly, "with some years of experience, the marchioness is no model for a girl making her first entry into society."

"But you did meet her at the linen draper's."

"Who told you?"

"The marchioness herself."

Harriet could not immediately speak. It seemed an admission of the worst sort of hypocrisy men practiced. They could mingle with persons of every rank and circumstance, from prizefighters to opera dancers, while insisting that their wives, sisters, and daughters restrict their own company.

"When?" she asked.

"Tonight."

"You rail at me for what—a chance encounter in a reputable establishment, frequented by dozens of ladies of quality—while you freely meet this woman wherever..." She waved a hand at his flaming red midsection. "Dressed like a circus performer." Hot anger made her heedless of her tongue and carried her forward in the little room. They stood in the circle of candlelight, breathing as if from the exertions of a dance. She ought to find it disagreeable to stand so near him, but her senses reeled from the impression of his height, his warmth, and the charged male energy of him. He regarded her as if he were really seeing her. His gaze settled on her mouth.

Harriet stepped back first.

"I beg your pardon," he said. "I meant no insult. Only—"

Harriet did not let him finish. The injustice of the charge still stung. "Two days ago, you came to me as a cousin to ask a favor, and now I'm merely the careless governess unfit to guide your sister—though the worst thing I appear to have done is to meet one of your more lofty relations in a linen draper's shop. I think, Lord Wynford, our agreement must come to an end."

"No." The word burst from him. After a pause, Wynford spoke again in more measured tones. "I wish to continue our arrangement."

"I can't imagine why, your lordship. You appear to share the marchioness's hearty disdain for governesses. Except for your deplorable taste in waistcoats, perhaps you are the best guardian of your sister in London society."

"My habit of protecting my sister is of long standing, and old habits are not easily changed. I don't wish Octavia to be...frightened."

"Surely," Harriet said, "your alarm is out of proportion unless you fear some danger other than a broken heart."

She wondered at Wynford's fears for his sister. Her own brother had been utterly indifferent to her once she refused to marry the man he had chosen. Something quite different had happened to Wynford, something that made him overcautious in regard to Octavia, who would remain weak and defenseless unless she had the freedom to choose her own path.

He did not answer at once, but Harriet sensed that he had regained his equanimity. "Perhaps only the danger in a brother's imagination."

"Then what are we to do? You must realize that Octavia will not sit by the fire sipping cocoa. She is determined to hunt a husband."

"Do you object to letting me know where you take her and with whom?"

"Are you proposing to spy on your sister?" The word *spy* caused a curious look to pass in his eyes.

He shook his head. "Only to be near at hand if any danger arises."

"And you suspect that Octavia may encounter this danger where? I assure you such plans as we have for the next lecture and a trip to the Burlington Arcade hardly seem fraught with peril."

"You relieve my mind."

"Do I? You appear to have not one jot of trust in my ability to see to your sister's well-being."

He studied her face with a slightly puzzled air. "What is it about you that every time we speak I end up putting a foot wrong? I am generally considered a man of some address."

"Perhaps you do not often speak with those whose circumstances—"

"Stop." He put a finger to her lips.

Harriet's whole body stilled, focused on that touch. *Not fair,* she wanted to say.

His expression altered. "Whatever misfortune sent you to the Luxboroughs, whatever the world thinks of your position, we are cousins. We are equal in birth, and...more. In spite of my missteps tonight, I do trust you with Octavia."

He removed his finger. Harriet's lips tingled. Wynford complained that he felt awkward and unlike himself. What of her feelings? Why should her quiet body shake and pulse with awareness merely because he questioned her judgment as a guide for his sister? Absurd that she should let his words unsettle her. Her life was in order. It was precisely the way she wanted it to be.

"I beg you, Miss Swanley, whatever your opinion of me, do not abandon Octavia."

"Tomorrow, then," she said, speaking with all the steadiness she could command. "We go to the Burlington Arcade in the afternoon. I will do my best to see that your sister purchases a new bonnet in safety."

*It is the custom in our island to hunt each bird in its season.
In the autumn months and into the early winter, shooters tramp
our woodlands and moors in search of grouse, partridge, and
pheasant. Naturally, the husband hunter imagines that there is a
"Season" for the hunting of husbands. If, however, we consider
the parish registry of each church as a sort of game book, we
will find writ there in every season the names of husbands
bagged by enterprising young ladies. Indeed, it is only in times
of mourning or great distress that a single woman chooses not
to hunt.*

—*The Husband Hunter's Guide to London*

Chapter 6

A heavy fog darkened the sky, obscuring the park and the tops of buildings, when the ladies descended from Lady Luxborough's carriage in Piccadilly to enter the arcade. Shoppers escaping the gloom crowded the long, narrow passage bright with lamps and light cast from shop windows. Camille, Anne, and Octavia linked arms and led the way, stopping at each shop window to exclaim over piles of pale macaroons and displays of delicate ivory fans and gloves of every shade.

Harriet could see no danger in the situation. Though ladies and a few gentlemen crowded the long covered passageway between the shops, the presence of the uniformed beadles in their stately blue frock coats and top hats insured order. No whistling or singing was permitted in the arcade, to discourage pickpockets and prostitutes from signaling to one another when a victim had been spotted.

A lively discussion was in progress about the nature of the hat Octavia meant to buy. Octavia quoted her guidebook about the importance of a young lady's being noticed and described the ribbons and feathers she had admired on the marchioness's bronze silk bonnet. Anne and Camille were quick to offer contrary opinions.

"Oh, but you don't want people to notice your hat. You want them to notice *you*," said Anne.

"Besides," said Camille, "your eyes are your best feature, so you don't want a hat that distracts from your face."

Octavia looked doubtful, but she said no more.

"Don't worry," said Anne. "There will be lots of hats to choose from. Oh, look, Harriet, shawls. Your favorite."

Harriet turned to the window Anne indicated. Shawls were truly her weakness. She kept to plain colors and fabrics for her gowns—dove grays, dark blues, and nut browns—but handwoven shawls from the distant East, with their vivid colors and formal designs, drew her. In the window, lying across a yellow damask sofa, was a stunning shawl of the deepest blue with a border of the curved *buta* design of the Mughal rulers of India embroidered in rich reds and golds.

"You should buy it, Harriet. It's just what you love," said Camille.

And there it was—the little reminder that she and her girls lived quite different lives. They could purchase whatever took their fancy and forget it in a week. She could not.

"I think I shall just admire it a moment longer," Harriet said.

"We'll take Octavia to Duddell's," said Camille. "They have the best prices."

"And we won't let her buy an ugly bonnet," added Anne.

Harriet nodded, still looking at the shawl. It was the deep cerulean blue that painters had once reserved only for the robes of saints, the blue of the heavens on a bright winter day, the blue of distances.

She did not know how long she had stood when a male voice at her side said, "Miss Swanley?"

She turned to find Captain Simon Mudge, a retired naval officer with a limp and brown military whiskers that curved along his jaw from his ears to his chin. She had met him occasionally after Sunday services through her friend Margaret Leach, companion to Lady Eliza Fawkener. It was Margaret who had helped Harriet grow accustomed to the daily slights endured by women who chose the role of governess or companion.

Captain Mudge was a comfortable sort of gentleman, part of a group of avid novel readers who exchanged books and called themselves, as a sort of joke, the Back Bench Lending Library.

"Admiring the India shawls?" he asked.

"That blue one, very much," she said.

"Ah," he said. "Did you know that the pattern is the unfurling of the cone of a male date palm tree, the source of life and fertility?"

"I did not know," Harriet said, wondering if men saw beauty at all.

"I brought one much like that to my sister when I came back from the Indies," he added.

"She must treasure it," Harriet answered.

He nodded. "It is surely one of the wonders of the East that such beauty comes from the underbellies of shaggy, long-haired goats."

Harriet laughed. "I had not thought of the goats, only of the artist at her loom."

"His loom more like," said the captain. "Are you here alone?"

"Oh," said Harriet, looking down the arcade. She did not see the girls. "Please excuse me, Captain. I must return to my charges, who are on their own in a bonnet shop."

He bowed, and she stepped into the crowd. All she could see down the line of the arcade were hats and bonnets. Duddell's was near the garden end of the long passage. She told herself not to worry. Octavia would try on at least a half dozen bonnets, and Anne and Camille would not hesitate to share their opinions, so it was unlikely Octavia would purchase anything truly dreadful. Harriet meant to live by her principles of letting her charges make and learn from their mistakes. If Octavia bought an ugly bonnet, Harriet would let her wear it and judge its effect for herself.

She was halfway down the arcade when a hand gripped her arm and she was spun around to face Wynford. "Where is she?" he demanded.

Harriet looked up into his frowning face and willed herself to be calm. "She's gone ahead with Anne and Camille to the hat shop," Harriet said. "We're not thirty steps away."

"Admit it. You've lost her."

A gentleman pushed past Harriet, casting a glare at the two of them for impeding the walkway.

Harriet steadied herself. "Not at all. The Luxborough girls are with her. I gave them permission to go ahead while I looked at a shawl."

"Looked at a shawl, or met a man?" he asked.

Harriet gasped. He had both misread her conduct and assumed the right to censure her for it. "You have been spying, haven't you?"

"My sister's safety is at stake." His mouth was a tight line.

"Are you mad?" she asked. Maybe he was. He wore another absurd waistcoat, a pink-and-green flowered monstrosity. Maybe in the ten years since she'd first met him something had happened to unhinge his mind. Maybe being the brother of a much younger sister had encouraged the autocratic tendency of his nature. "Your sister is with friends. The beadles are on duty everywhere."

"You don't know that she's safe. You weren't watching her." He grabbed her by the hand and hauled her after him. There was no clear path forward, so they moved in jerks, with Wynford forcing his way through the crowd.

Harriet begged pardon of people who exclaimed at their rude progress. No harm was going to come to Octavia. Lord Wynford was going to feel very foolish when Octavia appeared with her friends and a new bonnet. Harriet hoped he would feel embarrassed from his lordly ears to his toes of his glossy, polished boots.

When the way was blocked for a moment, he turned to her. "Which shop were they headed for?"

"Duddell's," she said.

He nodded and pulled her forward again.

When they reached the shop, Harriet prepared to be vindicated, but the girls were not there. In a flash Harriet knew where they had gone.

"Try Parson's," she said. "Number twenty-six." Parson's sold Paris-made hats for a guinea apiece.

Back they went against the tide of shoppers.

At Parson's, Octavia sat on a cushioned bench, turning her head this way and that to see the effect of a close-fitting silk bonnet of the deepest rose with a delicate pink lining. Looking over her shoulder was the marchioness, and behind her stood Anne and Camille, looking anxious and guilty.

"Charles," said Octavia, catching sight of her brother and coming to her feet. "Look who we met."

Harriet felt the rapid alteration in him through their joined hands, a current of relief followed by guardedness.

"Marchioness," he said. He dropped Harriet's hand, but not before the other woman noted the connection.

"Your sister looks charming, does she not? How fortunate that I was able to intercept her before she made the fatal error of shopping somewhere dull and English. Do you go to Lady Throckmorton's tonight?"

"I do."

"I've invited your sister to come. Was that too forward of me?" She turned to Octavia.

"Oh Charles," Octavia cried. "You must let me come. Cousin Isabelle says Lady Throckmorton has a daughter just my age, and I will meet more eligible gentlemen there in an evening than I ever will going to..." Octavia's brow furrowed as some thought occurred to stop her speech. "Going elsewhere," she finished.

Harriet did not need the touch of Wynford's hand to know how wary he instantly became.

"Of course you may go," he said. He turned to Harriet, and she could not mistake the appeal in his eyes. "Provided only that Miss Swanley is at liberty to accompany you."

All the others turned her way. Harriet nodded. "Of course." She could not fathom why a woman of the marchioness's obvious worldliness wished to exercise her influence over a green girl like Octavia, but she did not like it.

"It is settled then. *Au revoir,* sweet cousin, until tonight." The marchioness swept out of the little shop.

Octavia bounced with excitement, throwing her arms around her brother and thanking him.

"Let's pay for your purchase, shall we?" he said.

Anne and Camille looked on helplessly. Harriet went and stood between them, taking their hands and drawing them out of the shop. "Thank you," she said quietly, "for helping Octavia to find a becoming bonnet."

"It does look well on her, doesn't it?" said Anne.

Harriet nodded.

"But oh, Miss Swanley, we could not stop her from following her cousin to Parson's shop," said Camille.

"And we couldn't tell her about Lady Throckmorton. Could we?" Anne took over. "Even if Mama says Lady Throckmorton is...well, is...not quite genteel. Don't you always say to let people discredit themselves?"

"I do, and I'm proud of you both for staying with Octavia and for your tact and reserve. Do not worry about her tonight. I'll be there with her."

There was a moment of silence.

"But tonight you were going to begin this year's Christmas ghost story for Jasper's homecoming."

"I forgot," said Harriet. She had. Her ghost story had become an annual game played over four nights with the children drawing cards to create a ghost and Harriet bringing the spirit to life with clues. One year the ghost had been a headless coachman, another year, a terrible, red-eyed hound. For three days the ghost wandered Luxborough House, leaving clues to his or her identity, until his unveiling and laying to rest.

Octavia and Wynford emerged from the shop. Harriet's gaze met his, and to her utter mortification, she knew what had made her forget the ghost game.

"Forgive me," she said to Anne and Camille. "I promise we shall begin tomorrow night."

My dear husband hunter, if you are not the first woman in the room to whom every male eye is drawn, do not despair. Do not lament a lack of guinea gold curls, high color, or a striking bosom. These attributes attract the male eye, but they do not attach the male heart. A great beauty, such as Helen of Troy once was, must, in a sense, overcome her striking features to win a man's notice of her more enduring qualities. The wit and charm of a woman of more modest looks may shine all the brighter in the eyes of a man who is not distracted by mere appearances.

—The Husband Hunter's Guide to London

Chapter 7

At the entry to Lady Throckmorton's overcrowded red salon, where a squeeze was in progress, Charles took a deep breath of air ripe with competing scents of pomade, perfume, and warm flesh. It was perhaps an unlikely place to recognize that the way gentlemen experienced bachelorhood differed vastly from the way ladies experienced the single state.

Having escaped from his hostess's effusive welcome and stepped back from the upward thrust of her hopeful daughter's stunning bosom, he realized that he had for years avoided such parties where a single man of any fortune was as marked a quarry as a fox in Melton territory. Yet, it was upon such gatherings that his sister now pinned her hopes of happiness. Through her hand on his arm, Charles felt Octavia's trembling eagerness for the evening ahead. On his other arm, in steady contrast, he felt Harriet Swanley's calm presence.

He surveyed the crowd of largely indistinguishable highborn ladies in shimmering silks and jewels and bobbing feathers. For the first time since he'd come of age and been on the town, the Season struck him as an odd matchup between gentlemen who saw marriage as a distant duty to family name and line, to whom a ball was as tedious as a discussion of tithes, and girls whose flimsy gowns masked their steely determination to wed. His sister's dream of a husband by Christmas seemed destined to end in disappointment, if not heartache.

Beside him, Octavia spoke in hushed tones. "How people stare. I suppose you know everyone here."

"Most," he said, "and I daresay Miss Swanley does, too." It struck him that to enter a drawing room with Miss Swanley's air of detachment was no small feat. She was the first woman he'd met who had resisted the imperative to marry or to change herself in order to attract a gentleman's notice. The oddity of it made him curious about her.

In the face of a dozen pairs of eyes turned their way, assessing dress and hair and jewels and placing them in the hierarchy of fashion, he was grateful to her for the few alterations she had suggested to Octavia's attire. A gown of straw-colored silk with a single strand of his mother's pearls around her throat and a sprig of deep pink roses in her dusky curls became her.

Miss Swanley's gown, in a shade between blue and gray, like a smooth silver sea, had very little ornament, neither lace nor feathers. The fabric itself gleamed softly, and it was the woman one saw, her light and pleasing figure defined by careful seams and tiny tucks. Beside her in one of Perry's waistcoats, he made a garish figure.

"Shall we introduce you, Octavia?" he asked.

Octavia nodded, and Charles led his ladies into the crowd.

His friend Briggs-Price approached them at once, raising a quizzing glass to examine Charles's waistcoat. "My dear fellow, what wager have you lost?"

Charles laughed and presented his sister and her companion and experienced a mild shock. He was forever meeting Briggs-Price around town, but as the man bowed to Octavia, Charles saw not the high-spirited friend whose tales of various larks drew a laugh, but a worldly man to whom he would never entrust his sister. Then Briggs-Price's gaze passed over Octavia and fell on Miss Swanley with a speculative perusal that Charles thought her quiet appearance hardly justified.

He steered Octavia and Miss Swanley away from Briggs-Price toward a pair of his fellow spies in the crowd, the newly wed Sir Ajax Lynley, the tallest man in the room, and his bride, the former Lady Emily Radstock, now his partner in spying, the first woman admitted to Goldsworthy's club.

Lady Emily took charge of Octavia and Harriet to introduce them to other guests. With a slight inclination of his head, Lynley indicated where the marchioness sat on a gilt-edged red velvet chair. She had drawn a little court of single gentlemen around her, including Edenhorn, the MP with a post at the Exchequer.

Lynley snagged a waiter and procured Charles a glass of decent claret. "So," he began, "is she merely a widow looking for a new husband? Or is she the Russians' replacement for Malikov?"

Charles considered the three bachelor gentlemen hovering over her. Each had had intrigues with women of the demimonde, but he thought none of them would choose such a dashing specimen of womanhood as the marchioness for the position of mistress or wife. They were plodding sort of gentleman, not without ambition for some higher position in the government or the party but with a strong aversion for risk.

"No one in that group is going to propose to so bold a woman," he said. Whether any of them could resist her seduction if she set out to seduce him was another matter.

"Ah," said Lynley, grinning at him. "I didn't think so, but do any of them have access to the kind of information the Russians want?"

That was the question. Charles did not think so. And if she was not after information, did that mean she was not a spy? "That's my cue," he said.

It was his job to observe where she went in society and to note the connections she made. Outside of the ballrooms and salons of the fashionable world, she would be followed by another sort of spy, one who could move quickly and draw no notice to himself.

He looked round for Octavia and saw her in a group of young ladies with Miss Throckmorton. Harriet Swanley stood, aloof and cool, at the edge of the group. An odd inclination to go to her, stronger than mere curiosity, tugged at him. He owed her some sort of apology for doubting her care for his sister, and a less honorable part of himself wanted to test her air of detachment. But first the marchioness. His persimmon waistcoat had a startling effect that cleared his path.

* * * *

The evening seemed to Harriet designed to make her more conscious of her position as an onlooker rather than a participant in the great game underway in Lady Throckmorton's red salon. She had been amusing herself noting those details of the decorating scheme that confirmed Lady Luxborough's opinion of their hostess when Miss Throckmorton turned to Octavia. "Tell me about your brother," she invited Octavia. "He's not taken, is he?"

"Betrothed, you mean?" asked Octavia. "No. Charles is far too old to marry."

"Too old to marry?" For the briefest moment, Miss Throckmorton hesitated, glancing across the room at Wynford in the group of gentlemen around the marchioness. He was startlingly attractive compared to the others in spite of the waistcoat. "Perhaps he seems so to one used to country ways, but in town, I assure you, gentlemen of your brother's... age are quite...eligible."

"Surely, you would prefer a younger man," Octavia said.

"Oh," said Miss Throckmorton, "young men are such puppies. They adore you one minute and the next they go on about some horse or gun or the sort of wheels on a new sporting vehicle. Trust me, Miss Davenham, older men are much steadier. But if you don't mind a young man?" She shrugged. "I'm sure you'll find partners enough."

But when the dancing began, Octavia had no partner and endured the first two sets in mortification at Harriet's side among the chaperones. Across the room, Wynford in his carroty waistcoat continued to make himself agreeable to the marchioness. He did not look their way once.

At the end of a nearly interminable third set with Octavia slumping in the little gilt chair, Harriet told her charge to keep smiling and hold her head up a few moments longer. She made her way as discreetly as possible around the salon to Wynford's side and tugged his sleeve.

"Is wearing that waistcoat a penance for the fashion sins of your youth? Did you once wear yellow pantaloons and a Belcher neckcloth?"

"Miss Swanley?" His eyes told her he did not know whether to be astounded or amused at her daring to tease him.

She pressed home her advantage. "It would be most prudent of you to dance a quadrille with our hostess's daughter if you wish your sister to have any chance of a partner tonight."

She bowed and turned to make her way back to Octavia's side.

* * * *

Charles watched her walk away. Halfway around the room, she encountered Briggs-Price. There was an exchange Charles could not hear, some importuning on the part of the gentleman and, clearly, a refusal on the part of the lady. He guessed that Briggs-Price had invited her to dance. She responded with that cool detachment that made Charles think her position less a barrier than a shield against the world around her. He should ask Perry why she had left her home.

Across the room he caught Octavia's desperate glance. His sister needed help. With a bow, he left the marchioness's circle. An hour of listening to her mild flirtation with some of London's dullest men had not given him any more clues to her true identity. The too careful family tree and the reluctance to talk about the Delatour wines could be no more than the kinds of difficulties faced by anyone who had survived the turmoil in France. Her avoidance of Wellington still counted against her, but tonight she appeared to be what she said she was, a widow on the lookout for a man to keep her in comfortable circumstances in a world indifferent to single women.

He found Miss Throckmorton, engaged her for a set, and begged her assistance in finding his sister a partner. She was all bosom and compliance, and he set himself to be agreeable to yet another woman, while a small voice in his head whispered that he would rather dance with Harriet Swanley. Two sets later, with Octavia engaged to stand up with a chinless youth disdained by Miss Throckmorton, he left the dance floor and went to Miss Swanley's side. She listened—apparently with undivided interest—to the remarks of an elderly aunt of one of Miss Throckmorton's friends.

He bowed to both ladies and took the little gilt chair next to Miss Swanley. A waltz began, and Charles suppressed an irrational desire to pull Harriet Swanley out into the whirl, to see if he could break through her detachment.

"I must thank you," he said to her, "for recalling me to a sense of my duty to my sister. If, for any reason, I must leave the party, you will see her safely home?"

"Of course. I do not desert my charges, whatever you may think."

"Must I apologize for that remark?"

"I think you must."

Charles regarded her silently for a moment. He suspected that she owed much of her detachment to a lack of awareness of how a man might see her. "You seemed so engrossed," he said. "And you can't deny that the man was flirting with you."

"Captain Mudge flirting? He was explaining to me that the paisley design which ladies so much admire on their shawls is a fertility symbol, the unfurling cone of the male date palm."

"He was not."

"I assure you he was." There was a gleam of laughter in her eyes from which he could not turn away.

"He was trying to win you over with sheer erudition then."

"Oh paltry stuff."

Across the room, Octavia managed quite prettily one of the more complicated movements of the quadrille, gliding with the best of them.

"You are not so easily won?"

"Nothing less than a thorough knowledge of physics and astronomy wins me."

"But suppose he had offered to buy you the beautiful shawl?" Had he been in Mudge's situation seeing her look at that scarf, he would have bought the thing at once.

She looked shocked. "He would never do anything so improper."

"Ah, you think not. You think your position as governess shields you from the attentions of gentlemen?" The thought became fixed in his mind. He did not know what had happened to separate her from her family and put her on a course so different from the one expected of a woman of her birth and beauty. And she was a beauty. He had noticed immediately even in the bare yellow room under the stairs at Luxborough House. She could confine her hair in a style of severe symmetry. She could wear the plainest of gowns and go without jewels, but nevertheless, her eyes would flash, her smooth skin invite a man's hand to touch.

She studied her hands folded in her lap. He had made her uncomfortable.

"But I, too, must beg your pardon," she said.

"For what?"

"You are, I think, justified in your concern for Octavia. The marchioness appears to meet your sister with more frequency than mere chance would explain."

"I've noticed."

"If she is acting by design to influence your sister, you must wonder why."

"I admit I am puzzled by it," he said. He could not explain the instinct aroused by the marchioness's interest in Octavia. If the woman were a Russian agent, Octavia had no information. The Russians could not yet know that he was now a counteragent. Though each side seemed to discover the other's people fairly rapidly, the spy club had succeeded where the Foreign Office regulars had often failed, because its members were amateurs recruited from the ranks of gentlemen down on their luck, who served a year and a day. He and Lynley were exceptions to the rule only in that each had retained his fortune.

She pressed her gloved hands together in her lap. He suspected she was exercising a firm control over her naturally curious mind. He smiled to himself. He'd made her curious. She was not as indifferent to him as she appeared. It was a small thing, that curiosity, no bigger than a mustard seed, but he would make it grow. He supposed she wanted to ask why he took such an interest in a woman who made him uneasy. The easy answer, the one meant to disguise his true mission, was that he was a man and men pursued fascinating available women. "I know what you're thinking," he said.

"I imagine not," was her answer.

"Everyone finds her charming, but you don't like her," he said.

"She doesn't like me. She has a poor opinion of the English governess as a breed and claims superiority for our French counterparts." She offered him a wry smile. "You must not trust the judgment of a person who's been offended."

"But you are generally regarded as fair-minded, are you not?"

She laughed. "I'm not sure I can be in this instance, but you need not rely on my judgment. You could...I don't know...take the bull by the horns, and invite her to the theater with you and Octavia and judge for yourself what the marchioness's motives are."

It was a brilliant idea. He should have thought of it himself. He might catch the marchioness in more slips, but what made the plan appealing was the chance to work on Miss Swanley's resistance.

"Would you come with us?" he asked. He gave her a sideways glance, watching the play of emotion in her quiet face.

"Would that not defeat the purpose?" she asked.

It was just the opening he'd hoped for, the seed falling in a crack in the garden walk and sprouting a frail green shoot. "Not at all."

A temptation the husband hunter must avoid is unnecessary comparison with other young ladies. While she may wonder at another woman's success in attracting beaux, husband hunting is not a numbers game. The aim is not to entertain the attentions of many gentlemen but to win the steadfast affection of one man.

—*The Husband Hunter's Guide to London*

Chapter 8

In the end Harriet did see Octavia home. Wynford left the party just after midnight in the wake of the marchioness while Lady Throckmorton's guests were at supper. In the close darkness of the carriage, Octavia could not sit still. The cold was biting in spite of hot bricks under their feet and a blanket over their legs.

"Are you worried about your brother?" Harriet asked. She wondered whether Octavia felt deserted by Wynford's pursuit of the marchioness.

"Charles? No. I am trying to figure out how Miss Throckmorton does it." Octavia stuffed her hands deeper into her muff.

"Does what?"

"Has so many beaux. I danced as prettily as she did, didn't I?" Octavia twisted toward Harriet. "I didn't...bounce."

Harriet thought the less said about Miss Throckmorton's methods of attracting admirers the better. "You danced very well tonight, and you only need one beau, don't you?"

"Yes, but, I should like to choose, and I shouldn't like to have someone else's castoffs."

"Castoffs?"

"Miss Throckmorton told me that I could have either Mr. Povey or Mr. Paxton as she is done with them. But..."

"It sounds a bit like giving an old gown to a housemaid."

"That's what I thought." Octavia fell silent. The carriage rattled along in the dark. Then, in a smaller voice, she asked, "Does London change everyone?"

Harriet felt a quick sympathy for the girl. Octavia might not be able to name it, but she certainly felt the condescension in Miss Throckmorton's manner. "Has London changed someone you know? Your brother?"

"Not my brother." Octavia sighed. "Did you change when you came to town?"

Harriet tried to frame a careful answer. She had changed, of course, but not in order to hunt a husband. "I suppose I did change over time, by growing up and by living with the Luxboroughs. Lady Luxborough is a wise woman."

"I think I must change much faster than that."

"What would you change about yourself if you could?"

"Everything," announced Octavia. "My clothes and hair and manner of speech...everything."

Harriet smiled in the darkness. Octavia's everything list was shorter than she'd feared. It was full of changes that could be corrected and that would do no harm to her character. The wrong clothes could be abandoned. Hair would grow again. And affected speech was likely to fade away as Octavia grew more at ease in society.

"Must you change so much?"

"Yes, for I am determined to have a husband by Christmas."

"And you do not want a gentleman who loves you for...who you are?" Harriet surprised herself by asking. Hadn't she abandoned that idea long ago?

"I don't think love has anything to do with it."

"Can you wait a day or two to change everything?"

"Why?"

"Because tomorrow, there's a skating party to Hadleigh Pond. There will be any number of young gentlemen there, but probably not Miss Throckmorton."

* * * *

Shortly after dawn, Charles reported to Goldsworthy, the spymaster. He slipped into the Pantheon Club, just doors from Byron's famous publisher and the Royal Institution. The club's façade, concealed behind scaffolding and flapping canvas, gave it the appearance of one of the king's architectural projects, now abandoned. Most Londoners walked past the place, little dreaming it housed a spy organization. The club's other entrance was equally concealed by a modest chemist's shop in Bond Street.

Inside, the place offered all the comforts of a gentleman's club. The spacious coffee room with its high curved ceiling and carpeted floors was furnished with long couches and coffee superior to any he'd had in

London, except in the company of Sir George Fawkener, an agent returned from the East who had helped to brief Charles for his mission.

Nate Wilde, the club's majordomo, met him at the door, took his hat and coat, and offered a cup of the club's excellent brew. Wilde was a youth in his early twenties with something of London's East End rookeries in his face, a look at odds with his gentlemanly accent and tailoring. The tailoring, Charles knew, came from Kirby, the so-called chemist, who made elegant coats for the spies in the back of the shop on Bond Street—as well as the gaudy waistcoats Charles wore for his current assignment.

"The big man is ready for you, my lord," Wilde told him.

Charles swallowed a fortifying gulp of coffee and headed up the stairs. At his knock and Goldsworthy's gruff reply, Charles entered. In Goldsworthy's office, all disguise of a mere club was dropped. Cabinets of files, maps, and weapons suitable for the headquarters of a military operation lined two walls, and Goldsworthy's desk in front of the canvas-shrouded windows, always buried in loose papers, commanded the room like the brig of a warship.

Goldsworthy lifted his shaggy russet head. "Well, lad, have you sorted out the marchioness yet?" He waved a large hand toward one of the two green leather chairs facing his desk.

Charles took the indicated seat. "She's sniffing around Edenhorn a bit, but she's taken none of the bait."

"If she's not interested in information, what is she after?" Goldsworthy asked. He was a towering figure of a man, dressed in a rather old-fashioned brown frock coat and green waistcoat. In his similarity to an ancient, lichen-covered oak, he looked out of place behind a desk.

"She hasn't tipped her hand so far. Except…"

"Except?"

"She takes a curious interest in my sister."

"Your sister?" Goldsworthy's gaze turned sharp. "The one you keep in the country?"

"Unexpectedly, Octavia turned up on my doorstep this week."

Goldsworthy shook his head, frowning. "Not the plan, lad. Where is she staying?"

"With me, but I've secured a companion for her, a sort of governess. I've not let her alone."

Goldsworthy began to move the papers about on his desk, a restless habit to which Charles had grown accustomed. It meant the big man was thinking, reading the cards like a player who knows everything that's been dealt. Charles had learned a bit about him from Lynley. Goldsworthy had several networks of informants. The man himself could not operate in fashionable society, but he had ways of knowing the doings of scores of people. And he had a gift for spotting men like Charles, who were right for the job of counteragent.

When Charles had first learned who his predecessors in the club had been—Blackstone, Hazelwood, and Clare—he had not connected himself with them. Blackstone and Hazelwood had been recruited to spying from debt and disgrace. Clare had been a faded war hero watching helplessly as his wastrel older brother ruined the family estate. Charles, with his spotless reputation and thriving estates, was puzzled to find himself chosen for the club's year-and-a-day contract.

But Charles was an analyst. That's what he did, he analyzed, and he kept at it until the deeper pattern of Goldsworthy's choices became clear. He saw the thing that made him one of the band of spies: a lack of attachments.

Goldsworthy's previous spies had all been extraordinarily detached from that web of cordial connections that most London gentlemen took for granted, the ties of family and friends. Charles was indeed one of them. He led a London life of surfaces, of skimming across a frozen pond, and that was why he'd been recruited. He had no one to lose. Except, he had discovered, that one deep attachment that he'd kept hidden from the world—his sister.

The paper rustling stopped. Charles faced Goldsworthy's stare. There was something else about the list of former spies that eluded him, but he would analyze that later.

"You have a plan?" Goldsworthy asked.

"I have invited the marchioness to the theater with my sister." He did not need to mention that Harriet Swanley had put the idea into his head or that her presence was necessary to his interest in the plan.

* * * *

The scene at Hadleigh Pond seemed to lift Octavia's spirits after the disappointments of the Throckmorton party the night before. The fine, cold winter day had just enough of a breeze to bring a blush up in the cheeks. The narrow pond, nestled in a wooded hollow, was perhaps a hundred yards long. Leafless elms towered overhead. Several parties of young people had taken to the ice, and both the young gentlemen and ladies greeted the Luxborough party's arrival with shouts and encouraging cries. While the young men skated with brooms, brushing piles of snow and scattered leaves from the ice, Octavia, Anne, and Camille sat on a blanket-covered log at the pond's edge. Jasper dropped his skates and tried to bring Cat to order, but the dog ran a circle round the edge of the pond, sending birds squawking up from reeds and brush.

Octavia sat fitting the wooden skates to her boots and adjusting the leather straps that would hold them in place. She wore a bright red wool pelisse. "It's just like a bad ball," she lamented. "There are more ladies than gentlemen."

"Fortunately," said Harriet, "skating does not require that a gentleman ask a lady to stand up with him. Did you skate with a partner at home in Hampshire?" she asked. She recognized Octavia's way of hinting at the hurt that troubled her.

The dog came panting up to them and laid his head on Octavia's knee. She rubbed the silky head, ignoring Harriet's question. Then she pushed up from the log. Cat jumped up in anticipation of play, but she told him no and headed for the pond with determined strides. John Jowers, seeing her, skated over to offer a hand. Octavia thanked him but refused the hand, reached the pond, and then with easy grace took to the ice. Within minutes she was circling the pond in fine style. When Ned Luxborough offered her a broom, she accepted and joined the young men in clearing the ice. John Jowers stood transfixed until Anne and Camille called for help.

The skaters made a perfect winter scene in their bright woolen scarves and gloves against the ice and the bare black branches of the trees. For a few minutes Octavia seemed to forget her husband hunt as she spun and skimmed over the ice in great looping arcs. Anne and Camille clung laughing on wobbly legs to John Jowers's arms. The Rivers girls took turns partnering with Ned, and several other girls, unknown to Harriet, found willing teachers in the crowd.

The scene reminded Harriet of her own country childhood, of her old groom teaching her to skate. It was a small winter pleasure among dozens. She hadn't thought of skating as something to be missed. The air was still invigorating. The landscape pared down to its bare bones was lovely. She had come to Hadleigh Pond with the Luxborough children before and not felt deprived as her charges took to the ice. Only Octavia's pursuit of a husband changed everything, reminding Harriet of the path she had refused to take.

She had gone from girlhood to responsibility with no interval of giddy pleasure or romantic folly in between. She shook herself. She would be foolish to lament that now merely because she was doing a favor for Wynford.

A deep-voiced howl from Cat made Harriet turn away from the skaters. The dog stood on his hind legs against a tree, letting out the unholy sound. Harriet looked up. Jasper had climbed nearly to the top of the tree and lay along a thin branch that extended out from the trunk, ending in a tracery of twigs and an unmistakable ball of green with pale gleaming berries.

Harriet berated herself for letting the restless boy out of her sight, but she knew the folly of urging caution at such a moment. She glanced back at the skaters, who had linked arms, making a chain across the pond. Octavia had been included and laughed with the others. The day could be counted a success, as long as Jasper did not break a bone when he took the inevitable fall, which his daring and the slight branch under him insured.

Harriet tromped through the snow to the tree. Cat howled as Jasper inched along a slender branch, which bent under his weight. He paused and stretched one hand out, almost touching the green ball of mistletoe. Harriet looked at the snow-covered bushes beneath the boy. The bare foliage between him and the ground should break his fall.

"Hallo, everyone," he shouted to the skaters. "Look what I've found."

The line of linked skaters turned, swinging toward the boy, Octavia at one end. Contradictory cries of caution and encouragement added to Cat's howls as Jasper stretched the last few inches and grabbed the thin branch from which the mistletoe hung. He bent the branch downward, snapping it and sending the mistletoe plummeting.

A louder crack followed as Jasper's branch tore away from the main trunk. He rolled sideways and tumbled into the snowy bushes below, disappearing in a great tangle of bare shrubbery. A moment of silence reigned. Harriet's heart pounded in her chest. The dog ran in circles around the bush. The line of Luxborough siblings broke as they skated for the edge of the pond and scrambled up the bank to their fallen brother. Octavia stood alone at the edge of the pond. Behind her the other young people paired up and skated on.

Then Jasper's hand emerged from the bush, holding the clump of mistletoe aloft. He straightened up, a long red scratch on his right cheek.

"You clunch. You could have broken your neck," said Ned, extending a hand to help Jasper out of the tangle of bush.

Jasper grinned. "But I didn't, and you all will thank me later. Look at this bunch." He held up his prize. "There must be a score of berries, enough for each of my sisters to have a kiss. And you too, Miss Davenham," he called to Octavia.

"Not me," she replied. "Mistletoe is just another Christmas fraud. A kiss under the mistletoe means nothing."

The others looked shocked at the contemptuous outburst.

Jasper turned to Harriet. "Can we hang it in our drawing room tonight?" he asked.

Harriet did not have the heart to refuse. "After you risked life and limb to procure it? Of course," she said.

Octavia turned abruptly and skated away toward the far end of the pond, against the flow of the other skaters. As she veered around a couple in her path, she hit a patch of ice that caught her skate and sent her pitching in a wild tumble, her arms windmilling as she fell, hit hard, and slid to the far side of the pond on her bottom.

It falls to women perhaps more than to men to be sensible of the impression attire can make. Though London is justly famous for the skill of its tailors and for a degree of male elegance one is unlikely to meet in any other great city, the husband hunter must be wary of any gentleman given to excessive solicitude for the knot of his neckcloth, the cut of his lapels, or the pattern of his waistcoat.

—*The Husband Hunter's Guide to London*

Chapter 9

Harriet had not intended to accept Wynford's invitation, but Lady Luxborough insisted that the ice-skating party firmly absolved Harriet of any further duties to the Luxborough children that night. When Harriet mentioned her promise to start the game, her employer merely raised a brow and told her the game could wait.

Now her seat in the back of the second tier box allowed her the luxury of invisibility in the great crowd. Under the lights in the vast red-and-gold interior, everyone seemed to be talking at once, and how the actors ever made their lines heard over the din was a wonder. Wynford sat in front of her between Octavia and the marchioness, giving Harriet far too much time to contemplate the set of his shoulders and his profile as he turned to his partners.

At the second interval he disengaged from the marchioness and left the box to procure refreshments. Harriet let her gaze wander the theater as she listened to Octavia chatter. In spite of the bruises to her pride and person from her tumble on the ice, the girl seemed in good spirits, her color heightened by excitement. Below in the pit were dozens of young gentlemen in black eveningwear and the scarlet coats of several regiments, some of whom looked up at their box. Octavia, who was leaning on the balustrade, sat back and vigorously plied her fan.

After a while she ceased. "How silly I'm being," she confided to the marchioness. "A gentleman might look at a lady, but without an introduction he will not come to our box."

"Did you wish an introduction, my dear?" asked the marchioness.

"Do you know that gentleman?" Octavia asked the marchioness. Harriet could not see the man in question.

"Captain Fanshaw, is it?" said the marchioness. "Would you like to meet him?"

Octavia nodded. "He looks...amiable. Doesn't he?"

"Well, we will have to see what we can do," said the marchioness.

When Charles reentered the box, instead of taking his place between the ladies, he came to Harriet's side. "May we speak?" he asked quietly.

She stood and moved with him into the shadows at the back of the box.

"Are you enjoying the play?"

"I am, thank you. It's my first time seeing the younger Mr. Kemble." She tried to be sensible in the face of the smile Wynford gave her. She was doing him a favor. That was the thing to remember. It was her duty to help his sister, and the one piece of Octavia's conversation with the marchioness that puzzled and troubled her was the marchioness's claim to know a young English officer. "Do you still think the marchioness is a danger to your sister?"

Wynford frowned. "I can't see what it is in Octavia's naïveté that interests her."

Harriet tried to read his expression. The marchioness's interest in Octavia was puzzling, though it did not appear to justify Wynford's anxiety unless there was something he was not telling Harriet. "That bothers you?"

"Yes. I have no illusions that a woman of the marchioness's experience finds Octavia's views enlightening."

"I have to agree."

An amused glint came into his eyes. "And you don't like agreeing with me, do you?"

"That idea is as absurd as one of your waistcoats. I think I can manage to agree with you whenever..." Under his gaze, her thoughts trailed off. It was oddly intimate to talk quietly in the dim recess of the box, away from the lights, concealed from their nearest neighbors by gilt panels.

"Whenever I might be right?"

Harriet glanced at the pair still in conversation at the front of the box. From what Harriet had heard, the marchioness listened with little apparent interest to most of Octavia's confidences.

"It is only that I wonder whether the marchioness is interested in Octavia at all?"

"What then? You have an idea?"

"I have been listening to them this half hour. The marchioness's interest seems to be in *you*. I doubt she listens to anything Octavia says unless she's speaking of you, and the marchioness is quite clever at eliciting Octavia's artless confidences."

"Really?"

Harriet nodded. "Any disclosure about you, however trivial, has her full attention."

"Such as?"

"Such as those waistcoats of yours, which shock even your sister. Octavia cannot imagine why you let Perry dress you in the most appalling articles of male fashion, which she knows very well you never used to wear."

He stiffened almost imperceptibly. "Did she share her theory of my fashion choices with the marchioness?" he asked.

There was a note of caution in his voice when he spoke. Whatever the true cause of his unease, he held it back from her. It was a reminder to Harriet that the sense of intimacy she felt only went so far.

Harriet made a light answer. "Only that she, like others of your acquaintance, fears that you've lost some bet and she hopes you will not drive away her prospective suitors with your eccentricity."

He laughed then. "Ah, so flowered silk waistcoats are a danger to her husband hunting scheme. Shall I tell her I will wear Perry's choices only... until Twelfth Night?"

"Unfair, my lord. If you tell her that, you'll make her despair of finding a husband."

"Hah, any fellow who can be driven away by my bad taste in waistcoats is a paltry fellow indeed."

He teased, as an older brother might, but Harriet thought he had come near to the thing that bothered Octavia. "Is there a suitor who has turned away from Octavia? You mentioned her childhood friend. It seems unlikely that she cast him over to look for a London husband."

The interval was coming to an end. The musicians tuned their instruments, and people settled back into their seats in anticipation of the farce. Harriet expected Wynford to take his place between his sister and his guest, but he stepped closer though there was no danger of anyone overhearing them in the noise of the crowd.

"You are too shrewd, Miss Swanley. You think rather the reverse, don't you? That Gresham has turned away from my sister. I hadn't thought it possible, but you may be right."

"If her former beau has deserted her, it would explain why she wants to change her appearance so completely."

"Does she?"

"Oh yes. She wants to change *everything* about herself."

He looked grave at that.

"But don't worry, Octavia's notion of *everything* is quite superficial. I doubt she will change her true self except in those ways we all change as we grow a bit older and wiser."

"You are not claiming to be old, are you?"

"Merely older than I was, which, you have to admit, is the natural course of affairs."

"Has she confided in you?"

"Not directly, but she does fall into a bit of melancholy whenever Christmas is mentioned. And the Luxboroughs are quite keen on Christmas, I'm afraid."

"We have never been a family to rejoice much at Christmas," he said. "And you? Are you of the Luxborough persuasion?"

"No. More like you, I suppose. Christmas passes like a happy scene in a lighted window."

"And you don't see yourself there?"

She shook her head. It was lowering to reflect that she, Harriet, had shut down that font of generous, trusting impulses that Octavia plainly possessed in abundance and had instead cultivated the detached status of an observer. "I'm glad such happiness exists. Remote it might be, like the North Pole or the great Saharan Desert where the stars are numerous as grains of sand overhead." She stopped herself with a short laugh. "I may never go there, but it is pleasing now and then to contemplate such places. The mind shrinks, you know, without attention to such things."

He gave her a searching look. "Is that why you go to the Christmas lectures?"

She tried for a careless answer. "To keep my mind from shrinking? Yes, I suppose it is."

"Charles!" cried Octavia. "Listen to this scheme. The marchioness is willing to take me to Lady Hardwicke's solstice ball, where all the most eligible gentlemen will be, if I have a proper dress."

"How kind." He shot Harriet a glance, his expression carefully blank, as if he saw nothing amiss in the marchioness inviting his young sister to a ball given by one of London's most unconventional of hostesses. "It just so happens that Miss Swanley has agreed to take you to the dressmaker's... tomorrow."

Harriet had an instant to compose her face before Octavia turned her way looking stubborn. "But I must be truly fashionable to be noticed, and I must be noticed. I can't have some fusty old seamstress put me in outmoded attire."

"You'd prefer my tailor?" Wynford teased. "He has an eye for color."

"Charles!" Octavia shuddered.

"Kidding," he said. "I think you'll find Madame Marie Rambert far superior to the usual dressmaker."

Octavia turned back to the marchioness. "Will you come with us, dear marchioness, to keep me fashionable? We shall make a party, shall we?"

An odd change passed over the marchioness's face from mild amusement to an unexpected frown of displeasure at what Harriet could not be sure. Once again Wynford had arranged matters for a purpose she could not fathom.

* * * *

Octavia and Madame Rambert held differing opinions on what constituted an appropriate gown for a maiden of twenty years making her first appearance at a major ball. The elegant little shop on one of the newer squares was designed so that gentlemen might wait in comfort on gilt chairs in a green damasked outer room while Madame Rambert dressed their ladies in an inner sanctum behind rose velvet curtains. Madame Rambert might have more experience dressing highfliers than debutantes, but she rejected out of hand Octavia's first three choices—a lemon-colored Turkish satin, a straw-colored *gros de Naples*, and citrus-yellow velvet.

For the first time in Harriet's encounters with her, the marchioness appeared ill at ease. There was no fellow feeling between the two French women but rather a palpable dislike. As Madame Rambert offered her choices for Octavia to consider, Octavia appealed to the marchioness for an opinion, but she never spoke. She simply shrugged or raised one dark brow.

They had reached something of an impasse with Octavia standing on a dais in her shift and pantaloons and Madame Rambert, with the help of one of her assistants, holding up a bolt of fine white tulle draped with Haitian blue satin ribbon and Persian rose trim. Harriet thought the girl looked extraordinarily pretty.

Octavia stared at her reflection with evident dismay, blinking away tears. "Why must debutantes always wear white? There must be something else," she wailed.

She turned to the marchioness. "You would not be so conventional, would you, dear madam?"

The marchioness lifted one black brow in a wry arch. "A bit of *frippe* does not disguise stale bread."

The little assistant gasped, and Madame Rambert spun toward the marchioness, whipping the blue satin ribbon off Octavia's shoulders. "*Frippe*," she muttered, striding through the rose velvet curtains. "Stale bread."

With Madame Rambert out of the room, the marchioness spoke openly. "Be bold, my dear, and you will attract a bold lover, one who will act before Christmas."

Octavia turned to Harriet. "Oh dear, Miss Swanley. I do not mean to offend Madame Rambert, but I must be distinctive. My guide says so. Miss Throckmorton is always in gold, and everyone notices her."

"Do you have your book with you?" Harriet asked. "What does it say?"

Octavia jumped down from the dais, pulled the book from her reticule, flipped the pages, and pointed to a marked passage. For a moment, Harriet thought the girl would not release the precious book, but with sudden resolution she thrust it into Harriet's hands. Carefully, Harriet took it up and began to read, leafing through the short chapters, surprised at the good sense in many of the passages. The book was an obvious antidote to the dashing Frenchwoman's influence, if only Harriet could prevent Octavia from misreading its advice. She wanted to ask how Octavia had come by the book, but the question could wait until they were alone.

She looked up from a page on the distinction in one's attire and smiled. "Very sound advice here. Do you have a favorite color, Octavia? Poppy, lilac, primrose?"

Octavia shook her head.

"Hmm," Harriet said. "But you don't want to repeat Miss Throckmorton or to be mistaken for her."

"Never." The wounded look was back in the girl's eyes. "I just want to look different."

"Let's ask Madame if she has something *different*." Harriet hoped Madame Rambert had been listening behind the curtain. She understood Octavia's desire to be transformed, to be other than one's old self, the hurt self that had felt the sting of rejection.

Madame Rambert returned, stiff with offended dignity and briskly businesslike. "We try again. You want gold. You shall have gold, but not like King Midas." She produced a bolt of pale, poppy-colored India muslin dotted with sprigs of gold and draped the fabric over Octavia's shoulder, layering over it a deeper velvet poppy for a trim. Her assistant held a gold braid against the velvet.

Octavia stared entranced. "What do you think?" she asked the marchioness. "Will your Captain Fanshaw like it?"

The marchioness laughed, but she did not meet Harriet's eye. "All the gentlemen will notice you in such a gown, dear cousin."

Harriet had no knowledge of a Captain Fanshaw in the Luxboroughs' circle, and the idea that the marchioness had already suggested a husband candidate of her choosing to Octavia made Harriet think more of Wynford's distrust of his French cousin.

"What do you know of Captain Fanshaw, Miss Davenham?" she asked.

Octavia continued to admire her reflection in the glass. "I know he is handsome, and I hear that he is brave, and amiable, and will be at Lady Hardwicke's ball. Apparently, he has no fortune, but as I have sufficient, his lack is no matter." She gave a little toss of her head, and at Madame Rambert's signal, stepped down from the dais.

Again, the marchioness avoided Harriet's gaze. Harriet had to give the Frenchwoman credit for cleverly steering Octavia toward the unknown captain. It was just the right touch to caution the girl against a man of no fortune, allowing Octavia's natural rebellion to see the romance in that. He might be an entirely respectable gentleman, but somehow Harriet doubted that anyone invited to the notorious Lady Hardwicke's ball would be quite the thing.

Octavia accepted the proposed gown, and the shop assistants helped her into her clothes while Harriet stepped through the velvet curtains to the outer room to arrange when and where the gown was to be delivered and who would pay for it.

She started at finding Wynford in one of the gilt chairs. He wore a grim expression and a startling robin's-egg blue waistcoat. He raised a finger to his lips for silence. Harriet nodded, wondering how much he had already heard.

Madame Rambert bustled out from behind the curtains. She bowed to Wynford, but her mind was clearly on the marchioness. Harriet sensed that she was controlling her tongue with difficulty. She remained tight-lipped until Octavia and the marchioness emerged, all smiles, and greeted Wynford, and he escorted them out of the shop.

Harriet turned to the dressmaker. "Madame, did you wish to say something?"

"I beg your pardon, Miss Swanley," she said. "But that woman makes me feel the Revolution did not go far enough. *Frippe*, indeed. Does she not know the name Marie Rambert? Does she think I am some country peasant selling secondhand clothes? My wares come direct from Paris, I assure you. I doubt that she does."

There was a little silence. Harriet had not appreciated the layers of insult in the marchioness's words. She had guessed that *frippe* meant some sort of jam or preserves, and had thought the insult contained in the double meaning of the word *stale*.

"Forgive me," Madame Rambert said. "I let my tongue run away with me. The dress will be ready in time for Lady Hardwicke's ball."

*On occasion the husband hunter may feel a great temptation
from the warmth or distress of her feelings to express those
feelings in speech or to ink them onto a page of hot pressed
paper and drop a line in the post. Perhaps she feels the
growing coolness of a suitor who has completely possessed
her affections. Now more than anything she would like to
understand how the gentleman's feelings have changed.*

*In such a moment it is fatal both to her pride and her
reputation to succumb to the desire to enter into an improper
correspondence. Her anguish is no excuse for such a breach
of sense and decorum. A much better expedient is to open
her diary, and there un-bosom herself of all the torment and
confusion she feels, blot the page, close the book, and leave the
letter unsent.*

—The Husband Hunter's Guide to London

Chapter 10

The following Monday, Charles received from the marchioness a note
of regret that she was indisposed with a cold and must rest so that she
would be able to fulfill her promise to take Octavia to Lady Hardwicke's
ball. He recognized the polite evasion and wondered what the woman was
up to. Spying was making him quite suspicious of his fellow man. Only
Harriet Swanley seemed to him open and honest.

With no obligation to the marchioness, Charles wasted no time in turning
his attention to Captain Fanshaw. A few questions in his club had turned
up the information that the captain was with the Horse Guards and had
a reputation for idle charm. His father was a general with a substantial
estate in Wiltshire. The younger Fanshaw was apparently a competent
but unambitious soldier. Riding through the park and looking smart in
his scarlet coat seemed to satisfy his desire for military action. No one
knew any great ill of him, but no one thought him worth much. When
Charles asked where Fanshaw might be found when he was not on duty,
eyebrows went up. Apparently, he had a favorite brothel and a favorite
club for practicing his sword work. Charles made up his mind to seek out
the captain as soon as he reported to Goldsworthy.

* * * *

Harriet, aware that a necessary interval of several days must be got through between Octavia's meeting with the dressmaker and the Hardwicke ball to which she was to wear her new dress, invited Octavia to the afternoon's Royal Lecture. Anne and Camille were to go with their mother to a lying-in hospital of which Lady Luxborough was a sponsor to bring the mothers and new infants a box of those items most necessary to a baby's care.

At the Royal Institute, the day's topic included a brief digression from the planets to Ptolemy's ancient methods for determining the relative brightness of the stars. For a moment Octavia forgot her woes to lean forward in fascination. Harriet found her own attention wandering. Her gaze shifted to every movement at the door of the theater, and she took herself to task for the idle hope that Wynford would join them. Really, she would see him soon enough to report her observations from the dressmaker's.

John Jowers abandoned his male friends to sit with them and openly stared at the girl rather than the speaker. At the lecture's end he told Octavia she must come to the Luxboroughs' that evening.

"Why must I?" she replied with just that mulish tone Harriet was coming to recognize.

"So you can play Miss Swanley's game," John Jowers replied.

"More child's play? Like ice skating?" Octavia asked, assuming her most worldly air.

"You thought ice skating was good sport, didn't you?"

Harriet smiled to herself. Octavia refused to admit any such thing.

With surprising understanding of Octavia's mood, John Jowers simply walked away.

"He thinks I'm just a schoolroom chit," Octavia told Harriet. "What game?"

"Come tonight, and you'll find out." Harriet smiled, but refused to say more. Octavia's curiosity was a sign of the girl's forgetting her misery and looking outside herself.

* * * *

Charles sat blinking at Goldsworthy as Wilde poured coffee. The youth called it "cawfy," the one word that betrayed his East London origins.

"Under no circumstances," said the spymaster, "can I permit you to follow this man. Can't have you jeopardizing the whole mission."

Charles controlled a strong rush of rebellious feeling. A rich vapor rose from the cup in front of him. He picked it up and had a swallow. He would rely on reason. "I must disagree, sir," he said. "Pursuing Fanshaw won't hurt the mission. More likely his actions will shed light on the marchioness's intentions, which have so far eluded us."

"Nevertheless, can't have you spotted, Wynford. You'll stick out badly, and you mustn't tip your hand." A prodigious frown darkened Goldsworthy's brow. Even seated at his massive desk, Goldsworthy towered above visitors to his office. With his shaggy russet hair like a lion's mane, and his broad person dressed in browns and greens, he reminded Charles of the famous Green Knight of legend who had come to King Arthur's court with his huge axe and challenged the knights to a contest.

Wilde cleared his throat, and the big man's stare shifted to the youth.

"I could go with him, sir, and with Kirby's help, we could have his lordship looking like...the lowest scum of London."

Charles looked at Wilde. "You mean I'd have to abandon my splendid waistcoats?"

Wilde grinned at him. "And your fine polished boots, white linen, and tailored coat."

Charles grinned back at the youth. They both turned to Goldsworthy. The frown had not cleared from his brow, but his eyes darted rapidly back and forth, a sign that he was thinking furiously. He reached out absently, one of his huge hands swallowing the coffee cup in front of him. Charles waited.

"I've no doubt Kirby can turn you into a pauper, Wynford, but you'll give yourself away the minute you open your mouth."

"Then he'll have to be a mute, sir," suggested Wilde. "I'll be his keeper."

* * * *

In the end it was hard for Charles to decide what he missed most about his old self, or which of the petty discomforts of his disguise irked him more. The afternoon was raw, and his ragged coat was no defense against the cold of a keen wind off the river. He and Wilde traveled on foot at a quick pace, and the worn boots chafed his feet and admitted the damp of every ice-crusted puddle. He reeked with what Wilde explained was a mixture of stains Kirby had concocted from garments borrowed from butchers' stalls and gin houses. Charles had thought the brilliant waistcoats a disguise, but he had not experienced the full meaning of disguise until he caught the looks of his fellow Londoners when they caught a whiff of him. Most people gave him a wide berth, but some offered insult as well.

He had never questioned his right to walk the streets of London. To accept the sneers and slurs of ordinary citizens with no power of repaying them grated on his pride.

Fanshaw and his friend spent the morning sparring, not with Gentleman Jackson, but with a bruiser who ran a similar, if less polite, establishment in Covent Garden. The neighborhood bustled with rude life. But even the Waits, the rustic minstrels offering raucous Christmas carols, refused to go near Charles. By the time he and Wilde had followed Fanshaw and his friend to a posting house in the northwest corner of the city, Charles's jaw ached from clenching it to keep from returning some measure of the insults he'd received.

In the taproom of the posting house, the tapster took immediate objection to Charles's person, but Wilde produced coin and a story about taking his mute friend to a place that had work for him. Whether the story worked, or sufficient coin persuaded him, the tapster let them take a corner table away from other patrons, one of whom was the captain's friend.

A fire warmed the room. Charles wrapped his hands around the pint pot Wilde shoved his way and lowered his head, hoping notice would soon shift away from them. He composed himself to listen. The posting house seemed a curious spot for the captain to visit.

Travelers came and went, grabbing a quick bite at a long common table before a waiter returning from serving one of the upstairs rooms drew Charles's notice as he addressed the captain's friend.

"High and mighty ways your friend's lady has," the waiter observed. Apparently Fanshaw occupied one of the private dining rooms with a lady.

"No doubt," the friend replied, "but no concern of yours, fellow."

The waiter muttered to himself as he turned away. "Foreigners."

Charles and Wilde exchanged a look. In following Fanshaw, Charles had not expected to meet the marchioness, but suddenly it seemed possible that she was the arrogant foreigner to whom the waiter objected.

The afternoon dragged on with the tapster sending suspicious glances their way and Wilde buying more pints. The captain's friend drank steadily and turned over a pack of cards until Fanshaw came whistling down the stairs with a handful of letters.

"Took you long enough," his friend said.

"Letters to post," said Fanshaw, slapping them on the table.

"She had to write them, I suppose. Are you now the marchioness's French lapdog?"

Again Charles and Wilde exchanged a glance. The woman was upstairs. There was little chance they would encounter her, but Charles kept his head down just the same.

"Nothing of the sort." Fanshaw called for a pint from the tapster and seated himself. "Your trouble, Digby, is that you have no gallantry. You could be the one helping a defenseless woman alone in a strange country."

"You trust her?"

Fanshaw grinned and shook his head. "Of course not. Merely doing a small favor in exchange for meeting some heiress or other."

"Have a care what you're about."

"Meeting an heiress? No harm in it. The marchioness simply wants me to do what I do best—woo a woman." Fanshaw raised his glass in a toast to his surly friend.

Charles found it impossible not to stare at the two men, fixing their faces in his mind. But the men didn't matter. The letters did. The marchioness had gone to great trouble to conceal her correspondence. In the ordinary course of a visit to a reputable London hotel, a visitor would simply leave letters with the host, who would see them posted. Charles should try to see those letters and not let the ugly suspicion that Octavia was the target of Fanshaw's intended wooing cloud his judgment. But the prospect troubled him. Fanshaw had the careless, golden good looks and easy manner that women found attractive. He doubted Octavia would recognize the falseness in the man's charm.

He rose slowly, his battered feet protesting contact with the stiff, wet leather of his boots, and shuffled forward. Feigning unsteadiness, he leaned a hand on the edge of Fanshaw's table. The letters lay facedown. Charles jerked his hand up, intending to sweep them from the table.

Fanshaw slammed his drink down, sloshing ale and pinning the letters in place. "You reeking pile of rags, what are you about?"

Wilde leapt to his feet and tugged Charles's arm. "Never ye mind 'im, sir. He's a poor mute. Doesn't know what he's doing half the time."

"You'd best keep him from interfering with his betters, then, hadn't you, boy?" Fanshaw raised his drink again and drained it.

The tapster hustled out from behind his bar. "I'll toss 'em for yer, sir. Not our sort of customer." He signaled to the waiter to join him.

"No need fer tossin'," Wilde said. "We'll be on our way."

"Be quick about it, then," said the tapster, turning to Charles. Charles lifted his head and gave them a look that made the two men halt.

Fanshaw stood. "What? You're afraid of this reeking shambles?" He grabbed Charles by the shoulder and spun him round.

Charles's left fist shot out, smashing into Fanshaw's nose with a satisfying crack. Fanshaw staggered backward, knocking the table over, his nostrils spurting blood. The letters slid to the floor. Digby jumped up, shouting as ale sloshed over his coat and breeches.

Wilde scooped the letters up from the floor and gave them a quick glance. "I told ya," Wilde said, "he's mute, not deaf. Best not to upset him." Digby drew out a handkerchief, dabbing at the ale on his person. The tapster helped a cursing Fanshaw into a chair. Fanshaw snatched the man's bar cloth and pressed it to his gushing nose.

"Call the constables," Fanshaw cried.

"No need," said Wilde. He dropped the letters in Fanshaw's lap and dragged Charles past the staring patrons.

Out in the cold, Charles and Wilde slipped into the crowd around a stagecoach disembarking passengers and baggage. They circled the neighborhood and returned to a shadowed corner from which to watch the inn. Charles clamped his jaw shut against the cold.

A few minutes later Fanshaw, handkerchief to his nose, and his friend Digby rattled off in a hackney.

The day went dark rapidly. Wilde related the names he had seen on the letters—an M. Merville in Paris, Edenhorn the MP from the Exchequer, and Horace Gresham.

"Horace Gresham?" The name startled Charles. Gresham was his sister's childhood companion, the young man the neighbors assumed she would marry, the man for whom she had such an attachment of long standing that her appearance in London declaring that she had to find a husband by Christmas made no sense.

"What's strange, sir," said Wilde, "is that the letters were not all written by the same person. The letter to Gresham was in a different hand."

"Different how?" Charles asked.

"Smaller lettering, good copperplate style," said Wilde. "Sort of schoolgirlish, I'd say, the way my Miranda writes."

Charles stood stunned. Octavia wrote just that way. If the letter Wilde saw had come from her, she had violated propriety, discretion, and family loyalty in a shocking way. She had put the marchioness in a position to embarrass them both. He could not imagine her doing it, going behind his back and trusting the marchioness to keep her secret. He needed to know the truth of the matter.

An icy drop of water from an overhanging eave hit the back of his neck, setting his body shaking.

"Do we report to Goldsworthy, sir?" Wilde asked.

Charles shook his head. "Let's wait to see where the marchioness goes."

Within half an hour lamplighters were at work, and the woman emerged from the inn, showing no signs of the illness she'd feigned in her letter to Charles but getting deferential treatment from the landlord.

She thanked the man and offered him a handful of coins. He thanked her, but, glancing at the coins, he offered a couple back to her. She hesitated a moment, then held out her hand.

"Happy to take these golden boys my lady, but not any of this foreign lot. Got no use for such as them here." The landlord dropped two clinking coins in her hand. "Ye see, my lady, ye've got to know your Georges. George the Third, that's your sovereign coin. George the Fourth," he hefted the coin in his hand, "that's yer two pounder. Ye'll know by the weight, if ye catch me drift."

She laughed. "Would that all men were so honest," she said, accepting the landlord's help into the coach. The landlord directed the coachman to the marchioness's hotel, and Charles and Wilde turned back toward the club.

* * * *

At the club Wilde showed Charles to the room formerly occupied by Lord Blackstone. A warm fire, a hot bath, and the attentions of the club's valet, Twickler, restored him more or less to himself, except for a flame-colored silk waistcoat and a sense of betrayal. His own valet, Oxley, would have fainted had he seen Charles in the disguise he'd worn in pursuit of Fanshaw. What he needed was to get his mind in order. He decided to report all the facts to Goldsworthy but one. At least until he looked at a sample of his sister's handwriting and had a chance to speak with her. How to approach the subject with her was another dilemma. He could not represent the evils of trusting the marchioness until he knew the truth about her.

An hour later Goldsworthy shook his head at their report. "I don't like it, lads. The woman's pointed interest in you, Wynford, makes little sense. There has to be more to it than your supposed connection through your mother's French grandfather."

"I agree," said Charles. "There are official channels for pursuing any property claims she may have through our family. And, if she's innocent, why the subterfuge of sending her letters through Fanshaw from a posting inn? Why not send them direct from Mivart's Hotel?"

"And this Gresham fellow is your neighbor, you say? Is she acquainted with the man?"

"Our nearest neighbor." Charles kept his gaze steady in the face of Goldsworthy's scrutiny. "I don't know yet what the connection is."

"The Frenchwoman's made you a target, but why? No one knows your role here. No one even knows you're an analyst for the Foreign Office."

Charles said nothing. Someone knew more about Charles than he realized. He had no particular reputation in London. He was a single man of good but not extraordinary fortune. He had not called attention to himself by any of the exploits of sporting or betting men. He had friends, but except for Perry, he kept them at a distance. He had not raised expectations among matchmaking mamas as a man looking for a wife. In short, he had called as little notice to himself as a man could, until he began to wear the waistcoats provided him by the club. His work as an analyst had satisfied his mind's need for activity in the way that sparring and riding satisfied his body. So how had someone discovered that he might be other than he seemed?

"Yes, yes," Goldsworthy continued. "I know the Foreign Office leaks like an old tub, but I doubt even Chartwell understands what you do, lad." He shook his great head. "This fellow from the Exchequer doesn't know anything, I'm sure."

"I have to agree on that point, sir. I've never known Edenhorn to take an interest in foreign affairs."

Goldsworthy began to move the papers around on the great desk. "Did the marchioness see you?" he asked.

"No."

"Good. Did Fanshaw recognize you?"

"No." Charles had a question of his own. "Do you know who Merville is?"

Goldsworthy shuffled the papers on his desk. "Inquiries will be made."

London at any season is a scene of unceasing activity in which persons of every degree of rank play a part. Before dawn, carters, bakers, drovers, night soil men, and countless cooks and scullery maids light fires, draw water, and haul necessaries to and fro in the streets. By day bankers, merchants, and shopkeepers occupy themselves in all manner of enterprise in the service of gain. By night pleasure seekers and thieves alike revel and rob, while soberer, more respectable citizens bank their fires, blow out their candles, and retire to bed. Such is the whirl of activity in our great Babylon, that without care, without a pause for reflection or some refuge from its assault on her senses, the husband hunter may find herself burnt to a cinder. A time of solitary reflection or a quiet evening at home with friends will restore her spirits and energy.

—*The Husband Hunter's Guide to London*

Chapter 11

That evening Harriet found herself under Wynford's scrutiny as the Luxborough children explained the game she had invented for them years before to pass the impatient time before Christmas. Lord and Lady Luxborough had gone out for an evening engagement, leaving the family drawing room to their offspring.

It was a comfortable room to which old sofas and chairs retired as fashions changed in Lady Luxborough's more formal drawing room. Two faded teal blue sofas faced each other in front of the carved oak mantel. Three armchairs of various styles and colors tucked into the room's corners offered cozy retreats from the group, and included a black-and-gold chair from the craze for the Egyptian look, supposedly in the style preferred by the pharaohs, with perching Nile birds above the chair back and seated servant figures supporting the arms. Family lore said Lord Luxborough had declared the chair ridiculous and banished it from the main drawing room. Harriet sat at the tea table at the open end of the room opposite the sofas. A fire burned brightly, and all the candles and lamps were lit, giving a soft glow to green-gold silk that covered the walls.

Wynford seemed to recover himself a bit after his first notice of her. He took a seat on one of the blue sofas, and the dog, who had been sleeping on the hearth rug, rose and repositioned himself at the viscount's feet. Harriet concealed her surprise at Wynford's appearance. He looked haggard and knocked about, a condition in contrast with his flame-colored waistcoat. The knuckles of his left hand, resting on the dog's head, were scraped and bruised, and his brow was furrowed with some worry. Occasionally, she caught him looking at Octavia with a baffled gaze.

The others gathered around the cleared tea table as Pris retrieved the set of well-worn game cards in a velvet box with a secret drawer. Harriet couldn't say exactly what had inspired the game. She had been new to her position and searching desperately for something to engage all of her charges together in the last restless hour before they could be dismissed to their beds each night. She had made the cards out of some stiff paper in her schoolroom supplies.

There were eighteen, in red, yellow, and blue. Octavia turned them over, idly looking at the sketches and words inked on the face of each card. In that first year, Harriet had encouraged the children to suggest items for use in the game. Pris, at three, had been proud of her suggestion.

Now Pris bounced a little on her toes as she explained to a bored-looking Octavia how the game worked. "Miss Davenham, a ghost will haunt us for the next three days, and we have to solve the mystery. First, we draw three cards—one red, one blue, and one yellow. Harry puts them into the secret drawer at the bottom of this box."

Pris turned over three cards, showing Octavia the drawings of a candlestick, an ear, and a coachman. "The red cards name people in the household, the yellow cards, objects, and the blue cards name body parts."

"Body parts?" asked Octavia.

"Yes," said Pris, "because the ghost is always lacking some part of his or her anatomy. Like his toes."

"Toes?" Again Octavia appeared mystified.

Jasper cried "Boo!" in Octavia's ear, making her start and turn on him with a frown. "Toes were Pris's idea. The ghost could be lacking a head, a leg, an eye, an ear, or a hand. Like the headless woman that haunts St. James's Park."

"A headless woman haunts the park?" Octavia asked.

"Don't be taken in like a child, Miss Davenham." John Jowers stood facing Octavia from the opposite side of the table.

Octavia sent him a quick glare.

"It's not a take-in," protested Jasper at Octavia's side. "Sentries from the Coldstream Guards have seen her."

"Right," said Ned with obvious sarcasm.

Harriet glanced at Wynford on the sofa. His eyes were half-closed; his injured hand lay slack on the dog's head. He looked bone weary, but his brow remained clouded with some concern he clearly could not ease.

"The object," said Jasper, taking up the explanation from his sister, "is to be the first to solve the mystery of who's haunting us this year." Though he had been a mere infant when they'd begun the game, at eleven he was an enthusiastic player. He flipped over three cards. "Is it the headless butler with the holly branch? Or the one-eyed dog with the cellar key?"

"But how do you do figure out which it is?" Octavia asked.

Ned spoke next. "Harry takes the ghost's part and speaks for him or her and leaves clues around the house of the ghost's presence. And each night we may ask one other player to reveal a card."

"You play, too?" Octavia looked skeptical.

"Never miss it," said Ned. At twenty-one, he was a year older than Octavia. With some university behind him and time in London, he had a confidence beyond his years.

"There are rules," Jasper said. "No fair asking the servants what they saw."

"And," said Anne, "every night at tea Harriet adds another bit of the story, and we take a moment to see whether anyone wants to make a guess. You have to get all three parts right."

"It helps to figure out why the ghost haunts us," added Camille.

"Is there a prize for the winner?" Octavia asked.

"Oh yes," said Pris, "there is a mystery package on the last day, and the winner gets an extra slice of Twelfth Night cake."

Octavia looked around at the eager faces as if she thought them all a little mad. "But you have more people than you have cards, don't you?" she asked, with a quick glance at John Jowers.

"We can pick partners," said Pris. "You and John need someone in the house on your side, in any case."

A bit of squabbling ensued, but in a few minutes, sides had been decided. Harriet observed Octavia's face fall as she was paired with Jasper while John Jowers was paired with Camille. Jasper appeared oblivious, John Jowers slightly downcast.

When everyone was ready, Harriet spread the cards facedown on the table.

Octavia called to her brother, who seemed to wake from his preoccupation. He stood and came to look over Harriet's shoulder. The dog followed and sat at his feet. Octavia had the honor of picking the three cards that would define the ghost. Harriet collected them and tucked them away in the secret drawer of the velvet box. Then, taking turns, they drew the rest of the cards until every team had a set of red, blue, and yellow cards.

While the players retreated to sofas and corners to look at their cards and plan their strategies, Harriet returned to the tea table.

"Living dangerously, Miss Swanley?" Wynford asked.

She looked up, confused.

He pointed above her head. And there was Jasper's mistletoe, tied with a black-and-white checked ribbon to the chandelier under which she now stood.

"Oh," she said, stepping to one side. "I think governesses are exempt from such forfeits."

"Are they? I had not heard that rule," Wynford said. "You misled me at the theater the other night, Miss Swanley. I thought you didn't care for Christmas."

Harriet laughed. "I assure you I began this game entirely in self-defense. As a new governess with too many charges, I had to invent an occupation to entertain them for the hour before bed."

"Is there a part for me?" he asked, his tone at odds with his avowed disinterest in Christmas.

"It's for the children," she said lightly. Across the room, Jasper spoke earnestly to Octavia, who stared at John Jowers and Camille.

"But you play, do you not?" Wynford asked.

"My part is merely to set the ghost loose about the house."

"Merely?" He raised a brow. "You mean you are the authoress of the haunting."

"It's harmless, a pretend haunting, with nothing of real loss about it."

"Except that, if I understand it right, the ghost has lost a head or a limb." His eyes smiled, but his tired face remained drawn.

"Or his toes," she said, making a light reply.

Her burgundy shawl slipped from her shoulders, and he pulled it back into place with his scraped hand. "I thought you preferred a blue shawl."

His hand did not linger, but the conversation changed, dropped into a lower, more intimate key. Harriet told herself he did not intend seduction. He was merely a man who noticed things—but oh, the pleasure of his notice was sweet, like a bit of sugar crystal on the tongue.

"This one was a gift from Lady Luxborough," she replied, giving a plain answer in spite of the feelings he'd stirred.

She changed the subject. "In the dress shop yesterday did you hear the marchioness and Octavia speaking of Captain Fanshaw?"

"I did." He turned a troubled gaze to Octavia. "How does she seem to you tonight? To me she seems to be enjoying herself without a care."

"She does," Harriet agreed. "But you appear uneasy. Do you have some new cause for concern about her?"

"Only the same one," he said.

Harriet thought otherwise and wished he would take her into his confidence. "You know, Octavia may not find a husband here among the Luxboroughs, but she will find herself liked without changing her character. It's the plan of having her go to Lady Hardwicke's party expressly to meet this Captain Fanshaw that worries me."

"Then say you'll accompany her." The appeal burst from him with an earnestness that startled her. He immediately moderated his tone. "You will be free then, won't you? The Luxboroughs will have solved the mystery of your ghost before the solstice."

How neatly she'd been trapped. The favor he'd asked of her days ago continued to grow and to draw her into the London society she'd left before she'd ever come out or been presented. "Yes, the family will have left for Hampshire by then."

"And you?" he asked, again in that low voice. "Do you go with them?"

Honesty forced her to confess, "I go a few days later with some of the other..." A travel arrangement she had not questioned was now galling to admit. She forced herself to say it. "Staff. Nevertheless, I should apply to Lady Luxborough for permission."

"By all means, ask Lady Luxborough," he said.

She looked at him with some suspicion. "You seem sure of Lady Luxborough's approval."

"Do I?" He drew himself up. He might be worried and weary, and a wince of pain might cross his face, but his assurance remained undimmed.

"What did you do to your hand?" she asked.

The question surprised him, but he recovered. "A bit of sparring, such as gentlemen do. So the game begins tomorrow?"

"Yes."

"I'll bring Octavia. You can tell me Lady Luxborough's answer then," he said. He bowed and strolled over to his sister.

Alone in her room, Harriet took herself to task. She plainly enjoyed talking with Wynford too much, and not because he sought her wise counsel about his sister. She was painfully aware of his unwillingness to share his true worry. She could talk to Lady Luxborough anytime about Pris's tendency to leave tasks unfinished, or Jasper's defiance of any rule offered to him, or Anne's dreaminess, but as much as she enjoyed strategizing about how to guide her charges, she had to admit that the pleasure in talking with Wynford had little to do with Octavia's husband hunt or the danger of her too-easy acquaintance with the marchioness.

Harriet took the three cards from the velvet drawer and laughed at the odd combination. The randomness of the draw was always a challenge to her invention. She laid the cards on her writing desk and began to prepare for bed, letting her mind wander. A half-dozen plots occurred to her before an image fixed itself in her mind of Lady Luxborough's Egyptian chair. She tucked the three cards back in their velvet box. She had an idea. The game was a small part of Christmas she could freely enjoy. It belonged to her and to this house. She would not let Wynford's presence deter her from devising the best game she could. In the morning she would begin leaving clues.

It is a sad truth that the world universally condemns
that gentleman or lady who seeks to rise above his or her
circumstances by what is called an advantageous marriage.
A most difficult position then for the husband hunter is that of
governess. The difficulty does not arise from the meagerness of
her means, the Spartan nature of her quarters, or the demands
on her time, but rather from the limitations to her liberty. To
be always in the society of those who are her superiors only
in fortune and to deny herself equal intercourse with them, to
content herself rather with such condescension and civility as
may occasionally come her way, requires extraordinary strength
of character.

—*The Husband Hunter's Guide to London*

Chapter 12

The following evening Charles tried to remain as unobtrusive as a man could be in a peony velvet striped waistcoat. Octavia left his side as soon as they entered the Luxboroughs' second-best drawing room. There was nothing in his sister's manner that indicated any uneasiness of conscience over writing to a gentleman behind her brother's back, and he still had not decided how to confront her about the letter mailed by the marchioness. He had shown a sample of his sister's writing to Wilde, who could not confirm that it was exactly what he'd seen on Fanshaw's table, but near enough.

Charles had some idea of asking for advice from Harriet Swanley and took advantage of the liveliness of the Luxborough party to observe her sitting once again heedless of the bright green branches hanging over her head. She gave no hint of the answer she had for him about attending Lady Hardwicke's ball. As the game players fell into conversation, he approached the tea table. Her burgundy shawl was firmly in place around her shoulders over a gown of muted pewter. She had the look of a lone winter bird perched among frosted berries, but the game revealed another side of her.

"I take it that you'll be seeing the marchioness later," she said with a glance at his stripes as she poured him a cup of tea.

"You begin to understand me, do you?" he said, suppressing a quick flash of triumph. She had noticed his pattern. That meant she was not as indifferent to him as she pretended.

She gave him a cool look. "Not at all. I've never known a man to use excessive bad taste as his principal lure in pursuit of a woman."

"In pursuit of a woman? Is that..." He glanced away briefly. It was part of his disguise that his attentions to the marchioness appear to be the moves of a man seeking a liaison. He could not at this point in the investigation suggest otherwise. "You've not watched male birds display their bright plumage?"

"Oh, is that what it is?" One brow arched upward, but she did not press him. The players then demanded her attention. His five minutes of conversation with her were at an end. She rose from the tea table, and the children made room for her on one of the blue sofas. As they gathered around, the dog found him and inserted his head under Charles's free hand.

Jasper announced that a broken teacup he'd found at the foot of the servants' stair had to be a clue, while the others dismissed the cup because the servants' stair was not where the game was played.

"But it has to be," argued Jasper, "because four of the potential ghosts—the maid, the butler, the coachman, and the cook—might use those stairs."

"Or you might use them to sneak a bun from the kitchen," Pris said.

Charles had to admire the boy's logic—and gamesmanship as well, since Octavia had revealed their cards to him, and Jasper knew that one of the ghosts he named was not in fact the ghost.

"I think Jasper has a point," Octavia said in support of her teammate. "Though I haven't played before. I think one should be open to new possibilities."

"An admirable sentiment, Miss Davenham," said Ned. "Who else has a clue?"

"I noticed something," Camille reported. They all turned to her. "I banged my knee on Papa's crocodile skin valise in the hall outside his door, an odd place for that old thing to be."

"I'm confused," said Octavia. "There's no valise in the game, is there?"

"No, but anything out of the ordinary may tell us something about our ghost," Anne explained. "I found a candlestick knocked over on a book on Mama's table in the library."

"The teacup is a better clue," Jasper claimed. "A one-handed man could drop a teacup."

"You dropped the teacup yourself, just to throw us off," Pris insisted.

"Did not." Jasper snatched up a sofa pillow and raised it over his sister's head. Charles snagged the pillow from the boy's grasp.

"Now, everyone." Miss Swanley called them to attention, laughter in her gray eyes. "Prepare to hear the phantom's words." She retrieved a folded piece of paper from her pocket, opened it, and paused. The children, even Ned, stilled, watching her face. Her calm expression gave nothing away. If she decided to abandon being a governess, Charles thought she might do well as a spy.

"Listen as the phantom speaks. My visit is friendly. Though you do not often entertain such a guest as I, no need to make yourselves uneasy in my presence. You must forgive my clumsiness as an old injury plagues me. I come only for a kind drop of your hospitality after years in my dry tomb. Your mother has a chair that suits me well, and once I sit among you, I'll be no trouble, if only someone will bring me what I thirst for most. Won't you let me in this Christmas?"

As soon as she finished, everyone began talking. Jasper immediately claimed that he had been right about the broken teacup being an important clue. Miss Swanley allowed them to pass around the paper. Then she called for their questions. Several whispered consultations took place before Pris burst out with, "Which chair does the phantom like? There are dozens in Luxborough House."

"Why does the phantom have a dry tomb?" asked Ned. "Doesn't sound like any place in London."

Charles could not help watching Miss Swanley's face. Her countenance gave nothing away, though her eyes danced with merriment. She even had him speculating about the imaginary spirit. But he was more curious about her. He had not expected the last line of the phantom's speech, the plea to be allowed into the feast.

Anne had a question about the phantom's thirst. Camille and John Jowers wanted to know why the phantom might make them uneasy, and Jasper simply complained that the ghost's clumsiness was no clue at all because all of the injuries could make the ghost awkward. Octavia shot an impatient look at her partner.

Charles interrupted. "I have a question."

Miss Swanley's gaze lifted to meet his, and her expression grew wary at once. She bent her head over the paper, refolding it.

With some confusion, Pris asked, "Are you playing, Lord Wynford?"

He wanted to watch Miss Swanley's face, but with all of the children's eyes on him, he focused on Pris. "Merely trying to understand the game. Is the phantom's plea to be admitted to the feast a customary request or unique to this phantom?"

Ned answered. "The story always ends that way." All of the Luxborough heads nodded in agreement.

"For that's the 'spirit' of Christmas, isn't it?" added Anne. "To bring everyone in out of cold and dark?"

"So," said Jasper, "your question doesn't really help us, Lord Wynford."

Charles thought the answer explained a great deal about the woman who had invented the game ten years earlier as a mere girl who'd left her home and come to a family that held each other dear and expected her to be content to serve them. She had been younger then than all but Pris and Jasper now. Her charges valued her but did not fully know or understand her, for they, who had no lacks, no unanswered longings, did not see what she lacked.

There was a bit more whispering before it was time for the players to ask for a card from one another. Again Charles watched faces, noting degrees of satisfaction and disgust as players confirmed hunches they'd already formed or grew more confused. Octavia was one of the latter. She had confided in him the cards she and Jasper held—the cook, the eye, and the cellar key. It was another sign of the cleverness of Miss Swanley's game that just the three elements immediately suggested a story, but it was her story he wanted to know.

Perry had had little to tell him about her except that she had refused to marry the man her brother had chosen for her. Hearing Perry's account, Charles remembered that Dunraven had given a house party to introduce his sister to eligible men, but a combination of distaste for Dunraven and the illness of Charles's valet meant that Charles had left the party without ever meeting Miss Swanley.

When the cards had been exchanged, the players again turned to Miss Swanley, and she asked whether anyone was ready to hazard a guess. They all looked at one another and declined. She smiled. "More clues tomorrow," she said.

The Luxborough girls said their goodnights. Ned and his friend Jowers, who sent Octavia one last glance, headed off for some other amusement. Octavia lingered, clearly still thinking about the game, and willing to challenge Jasper. She smiled happily at Charles as she apparently won some concession from her partner before he, too, headed off to bed.

"I owe you an answer," said Harriet Swanley at Charles's side.

He turned to her at once. She didn't look at him but at Octavia.

"Lady Luxborough encourages me to accompany your sister to Lady Hardwicke's ball. She has a low opinion of Lady Hardwicke, and a high opinion of you, and believes I should strive to assist you and Octavia in any way I can."

"Thank you," he said, careful not to smile at his triumph. "I am in Lady Luxborough's debt."

"You are," she agreed, still not meeting his gaze.

"By the way, I mean to win your game."

"You aren't playing," she protested, turning to him with a flash of those eyes that made him catch his breath.

"I'll make my guess to you and not spoil it for the others," he told her.

"If you dare. You could get it wrong, you know."

"Dare? You think I'll get it wrong?" He looked astonished at the idea and leaned closer, lowering his voice for her alone. "Try me. Your specter's a traveler whose favorite chair is that Egyptian monstrosity in the corner, which perhaps reminds him of his dry tomb above the Nile."

Her eyes widened, but she gave no other sign that he'd hit the mark.

"Until tomorrow night," he said, and went to collect his sister.

* * * *

At midnight in the crowded supper room of another great house, Charles spotted the marchioness seated at a small table, surrounded by her growing court of interested gentlemen, none of them in peony stripes.

As he approached, Perry made his way through the crowd bearing a plate of little iced cakes in one hand and a glass of champagne in the other. With his gaze fixed in earnest concentration on the items he held, Perry looked much as he had at school, slight of build and youthful in face. In a word, vulnerable. Years on the town had not hardened him.

Charles could not catch his friend's eye, as Perry patiently begged pardon of those in his path, taking care not to let the shifting bodies knock the plate or the glass.

Charles stopped when he realized that Perry's goal was the marchioness.

Perry stepped into the circle around her, a slight furrow knitting his smooth brow.

"Oh dear, Mr. Pilkington," she said with a laugh. "You must forgive me for sending you off on a foolish errand. You see that am perfectly provided for at the moment, thanks to these gentlemen." She raised a glass of champagne to her lips.

Perry, with his hands full, looked at the gentlemen around her and at the table covered with plates. Charles stiffened with long forgotten outrage. In the group around the marchioness were some of their old schoolmates who had once delighted in mocking Perry.

"Another time, marchioness," Perry said with a bow. He tried to back away but remained neatly trapped in place by her admirers.

"Drink up, Pilkington," said Sedley next to Perry, giving him a clap on the back that sent champagne sloshing over his hand. No one laughed, but no one offered to help. Perry blinked slightly, awareness of the trick dawning in his eyes. Then he simply leaned over the table and poured the rest of the champagne into a dish of macaroons. While the others stared at the floating macaroons, he slipped from the circle.

Charles waited a moment to recover a little of his temper. He did not like to see his friend mocked, but a ballroom was not a boys school, and he could not use a left hook against a woman. He had to wonder why Perry had been made to look foolish. When only two gentlemen remained in the marchioness's circle, he approached and made his bow.

"You've recovered from your indisposition," he said.

"Thank you, I have, though I regret we missed our outing. Is your sister well?" One could almost mistake her smile for warmth except for the measuring coolness in her dark eyes.

"She is and anticipates seeing you at Lady Hardwicke's ball."

"I am delighted. I will call for her in my carriage," she said.

"No need. I must claim a brother's privilege to show her off in her new finery."

There was nothing in these polite opening maneuvers to alarm either party, he supposed, yet he sensed the marchioness's alertness to their surroundings. It was a good quality in a spy, that ability to notice a great deal without appearing to attend specifically to any person or object. With smiles and a wave of a black lace fan, she dismissed the two gentlemen who had lingered by her side.

"What did you find to do with yourself without me, I wonder?" she asked.

"Nothing." He sat in a gilt chair deserted by one of her earlier companions. "I am a dull fellow, I fear. I attended to estate matters, did a little sparring"— he flexed his uninjured right hand—"and kept Octavia occupied. I had not realized the work it is to chaperone a very young lady about London."

"You did not attend the Royal Lecture as your little governess friend does?"

She looked pointedly at his stripes, and he realized she'd set a trap for him.

If Octavia had attended the day's lecture with Harriet, it would only take a little polite interest on the marchioness's part to get the truth from her. "No. Sometimes a man must put duty before pleasure."

"You must know a great deal to manage such things."

"No more than most gentlemen. I have a competent man of business to assist me."

"I don't suppose you had occasion to come across any family records that might help me establish my claim to the Saumur vineyards?"

"Would you like me to search more diligently?" he asked.

She tapped him on the wrist with the black lace fan. It was a flirtatious gesture, but he did not think her a woman capable of doing anything lightly. "*Diligently?* Such a word to use at a party. It banishes amusement." She shook her head. "People who know too much get old and wrinkly quickly."

"Old and wrinkly?"

"Oh, it's a saying." She laughed.

He made note of it, however. It was a rare, spontaneous utterance, the sort of thing that could give her away, if she were not the woman she purported to be. He supposed he had less patience for games with her because of spending the early part of the evening in the company of a woman of warmth and honesty. He hoped he had not undone the effect of his waistcoat with his talk about managing his estate. He tugged the peony stripes into place.

She engaged him then in reminiscences of Saumur. Did he remember the walled garden of the vineyard house with its moss-covered bench under the walnut tree? The best place to rest in the heat of a harvest afternoon. He did remember. Octavia had taken her first wobbly steps to his mother in the shade of that tree. What he could not remember from that time was any mention of this cousin.

"You were happy away from Paris?" Charles adopted a teasing manner. "You would not wish to be so dull and countrified now, surely?"

She laughed, but the dark eyes snapped with alertness. "But one always sighs for what one has lost, *non?*"

Charles could almost believe her. She was at her most plausible as the plucky little cousin who spent happy moments in the orchards and fields of the Delatour family far from the upheavals of Paris. But the malice in her treatment of Perry revealed the bitterness of her nature.

The music started in the ballroom, and the marchioness stood. Charles came to his feet.

"I must leave you," she said, "for I have promised dances to..." She glanced at the crowd. "So many gentlemen. It is what a poor widow must do." She gave a little shrug of her gleaming white shoulders. "But you will honor our missed engagement, soon?"

He bowed and went in search of Perry.

When Charles found him, Perry explained that he had been one of the marchioness's circle, trying simply to observe her in action, when a lieutenant in the Horse Guards had brought a message that a Captain Fanshaw sent his regrets. The news apparently annoyed her, and she'd sent Perry on a fool's errand. He thought she'd done it out of pique.

Perry shook his head. "I should have seen through her. Any schoolboy would have, and I'm not in the fourth form any longer."

"Pouring the champagne over her macaroons showed that. Nicely done, Perry."

"Couldn't have you giving her a facer, could I?" Perry grinned.

"No."

"Sorry I didn't glean any intelligence. Meanness doesn't prove she's a spy, does it?"

Charles agreed. "But there was something in what she said tonight. I'll have to think on it."

If she wasn't his cousin, survivor of so much instability and violence in France, then she must be someone else, and if Russian, as he suspected, then somewhere she had learned to hate England. She might have come to London in the entourage of the czar for the premature victory celebrations of 1814. Or she might have been in Paris after Waterloo in 1816, when 160,000 of the czar's troops paraded through the streets, splendid in their high, rigid collars and rich uniforms, with their distinctive turned-out kick as they marched. Someone might have noted a striking diminutive beauty with a dislike for the plain British soldiers proclaimed the true victors of the hour. Her careful avoidance of Wellington might mean that she had once come to the notice of the great man and did not wish to be recognized. Charles would go back to the old intelligence reports and analyze.

*The husband hunter must not forget that certain boundaries
still exist, which may not be readily apparent in these days of
the greater openness of society. Irksome as such boundaries
appear, they act to preserve the unwary husband hunter from
heartache. There are a great many young men of charm,
education, and natural ability who yet lack the means of self-
support without the favor of friends and patrons. In a ballroom
or at table the husband hunter may enjoy their attentions and
feel the distinction of being singled out by their notice. But
she must remember that the primary aim of such a man is not
marriage but a place in the world.*

—The Husband Hunter's Guide to London

Chapter 13

When Wynford entered the Luxborough drawing room the following night, Harriet saw at once that he wore a subtle gray silk waistcoat. His eyes met hers, and she glanced away. It should not matter what he wore, and she should take no notice of his coat or neckcloth or any other thing about him. Apparently, he had no plan to see the marchioness this evening, and he had seen how glad that plain gray garment had made her. She busied herself with setting out the tea.

Ned greeted the guests, inviting them to stay for stargazing after the game. "It's a rare fine night, and Luxborough House has a patch of roof just made for catching a glimpse of the Geminid meteor showers."

John Jowers drew Octavia's glance when he added, "It's the best time of year for them. We could see as many as a hundred."

Anne turned the conversation from the stars back to the game by reminding them that the phantom had been quite busy. She gave an account of finding a plate of dates next to her workbasket, while Ned told of finding a sack of roasted chestnuts, still warm, when he returned from his morning ride. The others had received gifts as well.

"Wait," Octavia exclaimed, looking at John Jowers. "What sort of paltry ghost is this? In the country, you know, ghosts give horrid yells. They rap at the doors, move the furniture about, and make noises like spinning wheels or butter churns. And you tell me your ghost leaves presents for everyone?"

"Yes," said Pris. "Always on the second day."

"The phantom left me a handful of pennies," added Jasper.

"Remember," said Camille, "our ghost hopes to be admitted to the feast as a guest. Here's your gift, Octavia." Camille handed Octavia a small red velvet bag pulled closed at the top with a golden tie.

Octavia opened the little bag and poured ten peppermints into her palm. "Well," she said, "I don't see how these gifts tell you anything about your ghost."

For a few more minutes the details of the ghost's gifts went flying back and forth, as the group tried to find some common thread among them. Harriet glanced at Wynford. He seemed to absorb it all effortlessly, and he caused her some confusion as he came for his cup of tea and under the table pressed one foot lightly on her toes. He begged pardon as if it had been an accident, but Harriet had to glance down to hide a smile. He was far too quick to understand her phantom, and she should not play games with him that she could only lose.

His brow remained furrowed, however, whenever he gazed at Octavia. It was clear that she, not the Frenchwoman, was the source of his preoccupation. Harriet resolved to ask him again what troubled him. She had agreed to do him a favor, to look out for his sister; that was her role in his life. And she thought she was doing it well. The silly old game among the unpretentious Luxboroughs was a great antidote against the infection of the marchioness's sophistication and Octavia's hopes for the Hardwicke ball and the unknown Captain Fanshaw.

A pointed look from Ned made Harriet realize she was neglecting her duties in her preoccupation with Wynford. She lowered her gaze to the tea table, her face heated, striving to turn her unruly thoughts back to the game. To be caught staring at a man was an inexcusable lapse in propriety.

Ned covered for her, saying, "I don't know what the ghost is up to with the gifts, but it's no use, Harry, you've gone easy on us this year. The phantom must be carrying a teacup and dying of thirst. One thing everyone knows about this house is that you can always get a decent cup of tea."

She looked at the grinning faces around her and worked to keep her countenance. She was slipping, distracted by Wynford and his...gaudy plumage. "Do you wish to identify the phantom, Ned?" she asked.

"No, he doesn't," said Jasper, "because he doesn't know what the phantom's lost. Anything could make him clumsy."

"But only a lost head would make us uneasy," said Pris.

"But the phantom can't have lost a head," said Octavia, "for then the teacup would be useless."

A brief argument ensued, until Harriet raised a hand for silence. "Are you ready to hear the phantom speak?"

They quieted, and she moved to the sofa, withdrawing the day's written clue from her pocket.

"Listen as the phantom speaks. Though I've my nose in the air, I often look down rather than up. When I tired of the Christmas fog and frost of London's Thames, I sailed for sunny climes. Feluccas brought me down another river running past the palaces of mighty kings and queens long dead, but unseen in the water's depths lurked a dreadful danger. Address me properly, and I regain in form what I have lost in substance."

The evening's hushed consultations and card trading followed until Harriet challenged anyone to hazard a guess. Looks were exchanged, but no one yet felt sure enough.

When the moment passed, Ned stood and cried, "To the roof."

While the girls put the room to rights, the young men brought up cloaks and gloves and hats and scarves. With everyone bundling up, and Cat dancing excitedly among them, Harriet sought Wynford.

"You're worried about Octavia."

He looked chagrined. "Am I so obvious? She does not confide in me."

"As she formerly did?" Harriet guessed. "Do you think she now has something to confide?"

He looked grim. "I will not burden you."

"Haven't I agreed to guide her?"

"To a husband," he said.

"Come on, Harry," cried Jasper. "We're ready to go."

They followed Ned up to the roof, and as they passed out into the frosty night, Harriet held the door, cautioning them to mind the icy slates and to stay away from the lip of the roof. Wynford came last. He took charge of the door, shutting it firmly on the dog, and taking hold of Harriet's hand, pulled her onto the roof. The sensation of being borne forward by his strength flooded her with warmth.

In some confusion she turned to see that her charges were safe. They had lined up like ninepins along a narrow flat portion of the roof, their breath streaming straight up to the heavens in the still, dark night. Ned had a hand on Jasper's shoulder. Anne, Camille, and Pris held hands well back from the edge, and John Jowers looked quite ready to grab Octavia should she slip. Ned advised them all to let their eyes adjust to the dark by looking north first.

Wynford leaned down to whisper to Harriet. "They're safe."

They stood a little apart from the others, the narrowness of the roof enforcing a closeness that strict propriety would condemn. Their clothes brushed at every point. His hands rested on her shoulders, sending warmth down through her. He spoke quietly in her ear, pointing out Castor and Pollux, in whose heavenly neighborhood the Geminids would appear. But she was thinking only of him and his quick, clever mind, and not seeing the stars at all.

Pris was the first to cry out. "I see Polaris and the Plough."

"There's Cassiopeia," John Jowers added.

"Look, a meteor." Jasper pointed low in the sky.

"Where?" was the general cry. Everyone looked, then everyone declared that Jasper was having them on. The boy turned his gaze south.

"Well, there's Orion, anyway. You can't say I don't see Orion. You can always tell him by his belt."

Octavia laughed. "You mean like you can always tell my brother by his waistcoats?"

There was a moment of stunned silence at Octavia's audacity, then laughter, Wynford's among the rest. "Have a care, Octavia," he said lightly. "A brother's dignity is not to be trifled with."

Harriet was glad that his sense of humor remained unimpaired.

As they waited for another flash of meteor, a violent thump against the roof door made everyone turn.

"It's the phantom," said Jasper. Then Cat began to howl his mournful howl.

"No ghost, then," said Ned.

"Quick, everyone, back inside," Harriet urged. "We don't want to wake the whole street."

Laughing, they descended. John Jowers and Octavia came last, engaged in an argument that Harriet could not quite catch. She turned her head to them and saw Mr. Jowers steady Octavia when her foot caught in the hem of her dress. He quickly released her hand and turned away.

Goodnights were said. Promises were made to be the first to name the phantom. The young men went off for further amusement, and the girls and Jasper headed up to their rooms.

Wynford returned briefly to the drawing room to snatch up Octavia's bag of peppermints. He came straight to Harriet. "Your traveler with the teacup is a duke," he said, for her alone. A shiver went through her as if only the two of them played at the game instead of a noisy crowd of careless young people.

* * * *

The next afternoon, as Harriet and Octavia took their places for the last of the Royal Lectures, Octavia averted her gaze from the group of young gentlemen entering the theater and made a great business of arranging her reticule and fan in her lap. John Jowers passed up the aisle with only a brief nod to Harriet, his eyes like Octavia's, resolutely looking elsewhere.

Harriet waited. It was plain that Octavia was far from the listless girl she had been when she'd first arrived in London but equally clear that she'd had a falling-out with her friend.

Octavia at last looked up, her chin held high, her attention fixed on the table where Mr. Wallis would soon begin his talk. The benches were crowded, and people leaned over the balcony above to observe the models of the planets on display below. Under the noise of dozens of conversations, Harriet heard Octavia sigh.

"Thank goodness this is the last lecture. I don't think I could bear another," Octavia said with frankness if not with tact.

"Yes," Harriet agreed, keeping her countenance. "There can be enough of a good thing."

Octavia turned the green silk fan over in her hands, opening and closing it. "I don't mean to sound ungrateful to you for taking me," she said. "It is only that..."

"You and Mr. Jowers appear to have quarreled."

Octavia lifted startled eyes to Harriet. "He understands nothing of a woman's situation," she declared.

"Nothing?" Harriet asked. She suspected that the young man had been guilty of plain-speaking again.

"He doesn't understand that ladies *must* marry. Gentlemen do not have the least imperative to do so. Just look at my brother. They all have estates or prospects. And if those fail, they have professions."

"How did the subject of marriage arise between you and Mr. Jowers?" Harriet asked.

"Oh, he was asking me about my plans for Christmas, and I told him, of course, that I would not continue long with my brother because I must and will have a husband by Christmas."

"And he did not receive that news well?" Harriet surmised. Though Octavia could not see it, the young man was plainly smitten. Harriet had no doubt that Octavia's intention to marry had taken him by surprise. And Harriet imagined that with his frank disposition, he had strongly objected without disclosing his own feelings.

"Not at all. First he told me that I could not possibly have a husband by Christmas because the church doesn't let people marry in this season of the year or without a proclamation of the banns."

Harriet kept a smile to herself. "Had you not considered those obstacles to your plan?"

"Of course I had, but there are special licenses to be had, and one can always marry between Christmas and Twelfth Night, which is still Christmas in its way."

"Did he accept your logic then?"

"No. And when I told him about my book and explained how the writer's instructions on how to hunt a husband are quite clear, he said the whole notion of husband hunting was idiotic."

"That ended the conversation, I imagine."

"Not at all, because I said he was the idiot for not looking about to see how marriage works in town. And then he went on and on about love, as if gentlemen know anything about love, which, I can tell you, they do not."

"Ah, so you have done with his friendship?"

"I have. He was never a prospect, you understand." She opened and closed the fan again. "He is handsome, I suppose, in his way, and he doesn't entirely lack intelligence. He does know his Newton, but really, he is just a distraction, like the Luxboroughs and the whole ghost game. It is good that the game is ending tonight and that they all leave for the country. I will have ten whole days to concentrate on my hunt. At Lady Hardwicke's ball, I am bound to meet other gentlemen as well as Captain Fanshaw."

Octavia squared her shoulders and, with a toss of her head, turned to the stage.

Last-minute arrivals, Perry among them, hurried to find seats. Nothing Harriet had heard from her companion explained the worry that preoccupied Wynford. Octavia might artlessly confide her matrimonial ambitions to Harriet and even to John Jowers, but such openness to friends would hardly hurt her standing in London society.

Perry made a breathless sprint up the stairs and slipped in beside Harriet on the bench. Harriet thought she might sound Perry out about his friend's preoccupation, but Perry was looking triumphant.

"Got her," he said. "Faraday's done it."

The hour rang, and the lecture began.

As the husband hunter seeks to distinguish herself from the generality of young women in her situation, she may imagine herself the heroine of a novel and expect that she must fight evil or face death in order to win the notice of a particular gentleman. While this author will never discourage the reading of novels, I must protest that it is not in battle or in peril that a worthy woman wins a gentleman's highest regard, but rather in her response to the trifling occurrences of daily life.

—*The Husband Hunter's Guide to London*

Chapter 14

Charles thought he had grown accustomed to seeing Harriet Swanley sitting at the Luxborough tea table under the dangling bough of bright green leaves and translucent white berries tied with checked ribbon, but tonight he found that the disturbing effect was increasing. She wore an unremarkable gown of soft, dove-colored wool with the burgundy shawl bright around her shoulders and appeared not to notice as he entered. Her attention was fixed on Pris, who stood at the table earnestly explaining something with rapid hand motions.

One of Miss Swanley's wheat-brown curls had escaped the confines of the simple arrangement of her hair and caught the light, but she did not notice. The tilt of her head and the steadiness of her gray gaze revealed something fundamental to her nature, her ability to give her whole attention to one of her charges without any self-awareness. Charles wanted that attention for himself, somewhere private, like a bedroom. He wanted to wrap them both in nothing but her burgundy shawl. The erotic vision stopped him, and he deliberately looked away to recall the time and place.

The rest of the Luxborough clan stood around the Egyptian chair, which had been moved from its corner to face the hearth, a padded footstool in front of it and a table beside, set with a teacup, saucer, and spoon. On the chair lay a package wrapped in brown paper and a red silk ribbon.

Jasper called to Octavia. "These are the last clues," he said.

"What's in the package?" she asked. This evening Octavia had insisted on wearing the most modish of her new gowns, her hair up in an elaborate plumed coiffure more appropriate to a matron of thirty years than a miss of twenty.

"Oh, that's the prize," Jasper said. "It's a clue, too, and everyone's had a chance to hold it, except you and John." He picked the thing up and handed it to her.

Octavia took the package, turning it over in her hands and giving it a squeeze. "It's very soft, and there's more than one item, I think."

"Give John a chance," prompted Camille on behalf of her partner.

Charles caught an awkward exchange of glances between his sister and the young man. Octavia dropped her gaze at once, color rushing into her cheeks, and thrust the package his way, saying, "Here." She turned and marched over to the tea table, pursued by Jasper, asking her what she thought.

"Shall we make a guess?" he asked.

"We won't win if we rush it," she said.

"But I'm right," said Jasper, pointing at the Egyptian chair. "Look. It has to be the teacup."

Charles watched as his sister struggled to compose herself to pay attention to the boy. In a minute they fell into their usual form of squabbling conversation, Octavia's air of sophistication fading away as she tried to persuade her partner of the flaws in his thinking.

Charles turned to Harriet Swanley.

She looked up, offering a cup of tea, her gaze mild and faintly amused. He had a moment of wanting to speak, to tell her that she had no business to sit heedless under mistletoe as if she were immune to the current of awareness that passed between them at every meeting.

Instead, he gave her one of his cards with the identity of the ghost written on the back and accepted the tea she offered him.

She read the card and placed it on top of the velvet box that held the answer. Merriment danced in her eyes. "Think you've won?"

"I know so," he said.

"May we speak later?" she asked, more seriously.

He kept his countenance blank through an inconvenient, irrational spurt of hope that she had some feelings for him.

"About Octavia of course," she said.

"Of course." He bowed.

Around them the usual confused conversation passed among the players before they settled on the blue sofas to hear the phantom speak for the last time.

Harriet took her seat on one of the blue sofas and invited guesses. Heads shook around the room.

"Well, I've got it," Jasper declared. Across from him Octavia frowned.

"Jasper," Harriet said. "Does your partner agree to this guess?" Octavia shrugged. "Oh, let him guess. It's just a game."

Jasper jumped to his feet, crossed to the Egyptian chair, and held the package aloft. "It's the teacup, you see," he said. "And it's the butler, because he must have order, and he's in charge. And," he paused, a triumphant grin on his face, "he's lost his leg!"

"Jasper, you clunch," said Pris. She held up the card with the butler on it.

"Oh." The boy tossed the package on the chair and sat down upon the floor. The dog thumped his tail and put his head on the boy's knee.

"Anyone else?" asked Miss Swanley. She drew the final paper from her pocket and unfolded it.

"Listen as the phantom speaks. I rode high and mighty in my time with power in my hand over all who served me. I never dreamed I could be brought to crave your kindness by a lowly loss. If I beg a dance at your Christmas revels, dear ladies, don't say no."

"Hah," said Camille, jumping to her feet with a triumphant glance at her partner, John. "We know."

Charles's gaze met Miss Swanley's laughing one.

"Jasper's right about the teacup," said Camille, "but it's the duke, not the butler, who is so lordly that it might make us uneasy to have him as a guest, and he's lost his 'grace' when he lost his—" She turned to her partner.

"Toes," said John Jowers. "But he gets his 'grace' back when you rightly call him by his title." He turned to Camille and led her out into the room for an impromptu waltz.

Everyone looked to Miss Swanley, who reached for the velvet box, opened it, and spread the cards on the tea table, revealing the duke, the teacup, and the toes. Over the heads of the others her gaze met Charles's, acknowledging his victory.

Miss Swanley invited the winners to sit on the sofa and open the prize package. It turned out to be two sets of stockings, one for a man and one for a woman, which made everyone except Octavia laugh. Charles watched the frown deepen on her brow. He might be wrong about what troubled his sister. Maybe it was not some indiscreet letter to their neighbor. Maybe it was the defection of this young man to whom Charles had hardly paid attention.

Everyone then began to talk about the cards and clues and how the phantom had both led and misled them. Ned and John Jowers prepared to leave. Pris sat on the floor with Jasper and tried to cheer him. Anne and Camille engaged Octavia in a plan to see each other one more time before the Luxboroughs departed at noon for their country estate.

From the door, Jowers looked back at Octavia, but she studiously avoided returning his gaze.

Charles became aware of Miss Swanley at his side. "You see," she said, "that your sister and John Jowers have had a falling-out."

He nodded.

"I suspect her real quarrel may be with you, but it is not my place to intervene there," she said. "You must address the situation yourself."

"I have been meaning to speak with her," he said, stiffening at the gentle reminder. He might have had a heated moment of madness seeing Miss Swanley under the mistletoe, but she had plainly kept her feelings in check. She could speak of the business at hand, the favor she was doing for him.

"Of course," she said. "Pardon my interference, but you do not want her to have any reason to doubt or distrust you when we go to Lady Hardwicke's ball."

"Must you be so wise and reasonable?" he asked. He reached up to the hanging boughs tied to the chandelier and slipped one of the branching stems free of the bunch. A gleaming berry dropped and fell to the tea table near her fingers.

She watched without moving. "Would you have me otherwise?"

"At least once," he said. An idea of how he might break down the barrier she had put up had taken hold of him. "Will you dance with me at the Hardwicke ball?"

"Dance with you?" Her startled gaze flashed up to him. "You are forgetting the nature of our...connection."

He turned the sprig of mistletoe over in his hand. "That we are cousins? I don't think I've forgotten that for a moment."

Her chin came up. Her gaze locked stubbornly with his. "That I am to be a model of propriety for your sister?"

"A keeper of rules and conventions?" he asked.

"Yes."

He disliked the firm conviction in her answer. "But you are not indifferent to me," he said.

"How can you say such a thing?" A quick move of her hand, knocking the velvet box of game cards to the floor, betrayed her. She straightened, trying for a composure that he could see eluded her.

"I am right, however. Give me two minutes under the stars, and I will prove it to you."

A flush rose in her smooth cheeks, but she only said, "Then I'd best avoid the stars."

"If you can," he said. It would be the easiest thing in the world to take her hand and draw her into his arms, but he checked the impulse. Everything around them held her bound to propriety. If she needed stars, to release the fire of her nature, he would give her stars. "I promise to speak with Octavia in the morning." He stuck the green bough through the top buttonhole of his waistcoat and turned away before the temptation of the moment overpowered him.

It is among family that one is first taught to love. The husband hunter may wish to reflect on the lessons she has learned from observing the degree of consideration and forbearance the members of her own family show in their relations with one another. As her acquaintance with an attractive gentleman grows, she will want to observe closely whether his solicitude for her comfort and pleasure is matched by an equal consideration of his sister, his mother, and even his aunt.

—*The Husband Hunter's Guide to London*

Chapter 15

Charles studied his sister across the breakfast table in the blue morning room. In the country she had enjoyed her food unselfconsciously, always willing to accept treats from their cook, Mrs. Mullen. Active and energetic, she'd never had the sylphlike figure aspired to by London ladies. She had a robust natural prettiness of dark chestnut hair, large light brown eyes, and smooth rosy cheeks. This morning she sat listlessly pulling apart a piece of toast. He had yet to see her take a bite. As he considered it, he recognized the pattern he'd been seeing in her in London with bursts of energy followed by slumps. He did not know how to account for it.

She'd been most at home among the Luxboroughs, playing their ghost game. He had promised to take her to see them off to the country this morning. He hoped that the quarrel with Jowers or the Luxboroughs' leaving might be the cause of her low spirits and not, as he feared, some secret burden she was unwilling to share for fear of his censure.

He put aside the intelligence report he was reading. After a good bit of analysis, he and Perry had decided that the marchioness had probably been in Paris after the Brussels campaign, and Charles had narrowed his search for her true identity to a group of young women, the daughters of three high-ranking Russian officers who had been in Paris during the occupation after Waterloo. At the fetes and balls and gatherings of the victors, these five women would have mingled with officers from every army of the alliance. And now those women would be the age of the marchioness. He was on the verge of exposing her, but before he did he needed to know the truth about the letter addressed to their old neighbor.

"Octavia, do you still wish to see the Luxboroughs off this morning?" She glanced up, letting a piece of toast slip from her fingers. "Oh, sorry. I'm poor company this morning, aren't I?" He looked pointedly at the pile of toast bits on her plate. "Are you planning to feed the birds in the park?" She smiled a wan smile. "Just not hungry. What was your question?" He repeated it.

"Oh, of course." She picked up the toast again. "Why do you think their games seem livelier than ours?" she asked. "Is it because there are more of them while we are just two? Or is it because they have Miss Swanley? She makes everything cheerful, doesn't she?"

Octavia was right, he realized. Harriet Swanley, however reserved she was about her own situation, fostered merriment in her charges. In their company her eyes flashed with quick comprehension of a joke. She seemed to understand them all and to have mastered the art of letting them go without letting them come to harm. He, on the other hand, had kept his sister safe by keeping her at Wynford Hall, and now saw only where her eagerness for the notice of the world and ignorance of London might lead to her embarrassment or injury.

He cleared his throat. "Octavia, I must ask you a serious question."

"Serious?"

"Quite. Have you corresponded with Gresham from London?"

"Gresham?" She said blankly. "I have forgot that name. You think anything could induce me to write to a man who—"

"Who what?" Charles asked, striving for an even tone. It was the first direct hint Octavia had given that anything was amiss between her and her childhood companion.

"Never mind. Have you been looking at my post?" Her eyes flashed. "I'm sure I've had no occasion to write to anyone except as politeness requires."

"I have not touched your post."

"What then?"

He hesitated, looking at the abandoned eggs on his plate, searching for the right words.

"Have you been spying on me?" she asked. Her eyes declared her outrage. "Surely, I may write to a cousin, to Miss Swanley or the dear marchioness."

"I've not spied on you. Quite by accident I saw a letter addressed to Gresham in a hand so very much like your own that my duty as a brother compels me to put the question to you."

"Your duty? I am a duty to you? That's why you fobbed me off on Miss Swanley, isn't it? So you could go about London in your ridiculous waistcoats flirting with women like the marchioness without the burden of a troublesome sister."

"You know you are not a burden and much more than a duty, but I..."
He could not mistake the wounded look in her eyes, but its cause eluded him. "I must protect you. I will always protect you."

"But not trust me, apparently. You didn't want me to come to London. You never invited me before. Now I understand why. Thank you, Charles, for making it so clear to me how I am regarded in your eyes."

"I thought you safer and happier at home. You enjoy country ways. You and Gresham—"

Octavia stood abruptly. "You are selfish and old and...you don't understand anything." She left the room. The door closed sharply, rattling his coffee cup in its saucer.

* * * *

Charles was grateful for the confusion of the Luxboroughs' departure. Removing a family of seven, their servants, and at least a fraction of their possessions from London to a country home in Hampshire nearly ninety miles away required a coordinated effort on the part of the lady of the house and her staff. Under low pewter clouds, two large coaches, their doors open, steps down, waited to receive passengers while three footmen milled about disposing of cases and boxes under the direction of the Luxborough butler. A groom walked the horses of Lord Luxborough's sporting vehicle, and in the noise of orders and farewells, horses and one barking dog, no one noticed the silence between Charles and Octavia.

The dog was not helping the proceedings. Cat was the first to see Charles and bounded his way, nearly knocking over a footman straining to secure a box to the roof of the second carriage.

"Jasper," cried Lady Luxborough, turning from Harriet Swanley, "see to your dog."

"I can't hold him, Mama," the boy replied. Cat sat expectantly at Charles's feet, a large stick in his mouth, a hopeful look in the deep brown eyes. "Drop it," Charles said.

Lady Luxborough shot him a grateful glance. "Jasper, put that dog in the yellow room until we are absolutely ready to leave," she ordered.

"Yes, Mama. Come on, Cat." The boy led the dog into the house.

Charles turned to see that Octavia had joined her friends on the steps and was studiously avoiding him. Miss Swanley appeared equally oblivious of his arrival, standing in the midst of the commotion, receiving last-minute instructions from Lady Luxborough.

Lady Luxborough, a tall, stately beauty with an air of affectionate command and a keen eye for the flurry of movement around her, appeared to be offering motherly advice to her governess. Charles guessed from the look in Harriet's eyes that the advice was being met with some resistance until Lady Luxborough said something that made Miss Swanley laugh.

He had come to appreciate the warmth of that playful ripple of sound. Playing the ghost game she'd invented, he had heard it often. He had not thought her free to share a laugh with her employer. He now saw a bond of affection between them. He had been thinking Miss Swanley an unhappy outsider in the Luxborough clan. He knew that in asking her to dance he was asking her to step out of the role she'd played among them for so long. Perhaps it was only his vanity, the vanity of an eligible gentleman, that whispered she was attracted to him.

The leisurely bustle of leave-taking changed in an instant when Lord Luxborough strode from the house with Ned and Jasper in his wake. Luxborough, in his caped greatcoat, whip in hand, paused to greet Charles, gave an assessing glance to the state of preparations, and caught his wife's eye.

She turned to him at once. Some unspoken understanding passed between them.

"You wanted a timely departure, wife?" Luxborough asked, signaling his groom.

A lift of his wife's fair brows was the answer.

"Jasper," his lordship cried, "with me." Without another word, he turned to mount his curricle.

Jasper let out a loud whoop and tossed his hat in the air, which brought a severe maternal frown. The boy recovered his hat and stood before his mother, who straightened his collar. Under her gaze he promised, "I'll obey Papa to the letter."

A moment longer that gaze held him before his mother nodded her dismissal, and the boy scrambled up beside his father. Luxborough set his horses in motion.

Ned turned to his mother with a laugh. "See you in Reading, mother," he said.

"Are you off, then?" she asked her oldest child.

"You'd best be off, too," he said as a second groom brought his horse forward. "You want to be ahead of the snow." He kissed her cheek, nodded to Charles, and mounted his horse.

Laughing, Lady Luxborough pressed a list of instructions in Harriet's hands, gave those hands a quick squeeze, and summoned her daughters. Pris came at once; Anne and Camille gave Octavia parting embraces and followed along. Lady Luxborough called to Octavia, "Do enjoy your ball, Miss Davenham. The girls will want to hear your account of it when they return, and do not forget that we give a Twelfth Night party, to which you and your brother are invited." At the carriage door, she turned to Charles. "Wynford, can you assist us?" He stepped forward to hand the ladies into the coach. As she entered, Lady Luxborough said for his ears alone, "If you do not dance with that stubborn girl at Lady Hardwicke's ball, Wynford, I shall wash my hands of you."

"I intend to, ma'am," he said. A footman stepped forward to fold up the steps and close the door.

As the first coach pulled away, two maids and his lordship's valet climbed into the second coach and a footman sprang up on the box beside the coachman, and it too rattled off, leaving Octavia, Charles, and Harriet standing on the paving stones looking after them. The shift from the noise and animation of the family group to the silence of the empty street was pronounced. He remembered Harriet Swanley saying that for her Christmas was a scene in a lighted window observed from the street. He thought he understood.

Miss Swanley's questioning gaze met his over Octavia's head. Something in her eyes lifted his spirits. She was not indifferent. He mouthed the words "not speaking to me."

Miss Swanley turned to Octavia. "Octavia, will you join me for some chocolate this morning? Your brother can collect you later if you like."

"Thank you, Miss Swanley." Octavia turned away with stiff dignity and without a backward glance.

Charles bowed and took his leave. Octavia was safe for the moment, and he had hours of work to do. Later, after he had sifted through pages of intelligence reports for clues to the marchioness's true identity, he would seek Miss Swanley and confess the way he had mishandled the conversation with his sister. If he had briefly had the upper hand in this game they played, he had somehow lost the advantage. He meant to regain it before the Hardwicke ball.

Neither marriage nor happiness is reserved solely to persons of a high degree of rank in society. The husband hunter whose rank has destined her for certain employments in society may as confidently seek a husband worthy of her goodness and wit as any duchess.

—*The Husband Hunter's Guide to London*

Chapter 16

Over thick, dark chocolate, Harriet sought to discover what had happened between brother and sister. She had done her best to avoid looking at Wynford, but in the midst of the Luxboroughs' family cheer, she could not miss the rift between the siblings and hoped she was not to blame for encouraging Wynford to speak to Octavia.

They retreated to the second-best drawing room. Some brightness had left the room from the night before when everyone had been in high spirits, but Harriet pushed the drapery aside to let in as much light as the overcast day permitted and set the chocolate and ginger cakes near the fire, which burned brightly. Jasper's mistletoe still hung from the chandelier, but she tried not to think about that.

Octavia wandered about the room, picking up a book from a side table, moving a vase. "You know," she said at last, sitting down opposite Harriet on one of the sofas. "I think that Charles should redo his house. His morning room is painted such a dismal, gloomy blue color, not like these cheery walls at all."

"This room always cheers me," Harriet said. "And chocolate. Will you have some?"

Octavia nodded. Harriet poured, waiting, letting the girl pick her moment.

"I suppose you have been with the Luxboroughs a long time," Octavia said.

"Ten years."

"Since Charles came into his title." Octavia stared at her chocolate without sipping.

Harriet waited for any further revelation. It was an interesting way to measure time, not in terms of her own life, but in terms of her brother's. "Did he leave you behind then?"

Octavia's head came up. She nodded and at last tasted her chocolate. "Oh, this is so good."

"And now?" Harriet asked. "I thought him very attentive."

Octavia put her cup down and picked up a ginger cake, breaking off a small piece. "But he doesn't know me at all, you see. He thinks I am still... as much a child as I was when he left home. He treats me as the merest schoolroom miss, and he thinks that because he protected me as a babe when the soldiers came, now nearly twenty years later I can't stand up for myself."

"Soldiers came where?" Harriet prompted. Wynford Hall seemed the least likely place to encounter soldiery, unless in those years of fear of a French invasion some militia had been quartered nearby.

Octavia looked abashed. "We do not usually tell the tale."

"Of course," said Harriet, quelling her impatience. A story was best told freely when the teller was ready. "I did not mean to pry."

"Never mind all that old history." Octavia waved a small hand in the air. "You must see how difficult Charles is being when all I mean to do is to take myself off his hands by finding a husband, which I can do very well on my own with no interference from him. I have my book, after all." Octavia reached for her reticule and pulled forth the little blue book with the gold lettering and held it in her lap.

"Does Charles want you off his hands?" Harriet asked.

"Oh, you may be sure he does," Octavia said. "Perry told me as much when I first arrived. Charles wants to live the single gentleman's life wearing his outrageous waistcoats and pursuing women like our cousin the marchioness. He wants no ties, no burdens."

Harriet looked at the girl's bleak expression and wondered how she had so misinterpreted her brother's behavior toward her. "I don't suppose your book has any advice on dealing with brothers?"

Octavia shook her head and tucked the book away. "But the book does advise a woman to know her own mind. Charles thinks I can't possibly know my own mind. He thinks I am still that infant who needed protecting."

Harriet sipped her chocolate, letting Octavia withdraw into her own thoughts. The pile of ginger cake crumbs grew.

"Just because I could not defend myself as an infant, he thinks I cannot defend myself now. He thinks I will be taken in by everyone I meet, by Captain Fanshaw, whom I have never met, or even by the marchioness, who is our cousin. But I am done with being anyone's dupe. I know exactly what it is to be taken in, and I won't let anyone deceive me again." She seized her cup of chocolate and took a hearty swallow.

"An excellent resolution," Harriet said. She was no nearer to understanding what had precipitated the rift between brother and sister, but she was beginning to understand Octavia's determination to rely on herself. She sipped her chocolate, trying to think what Charles might have said over breakfast in that blue room to set Octavia off. Before she could ask, Octavia began again.

"You know what's worse?" she asked, setting her cup down.

Harriet shook her head. She was inclined to agree with Octavia that Wynford was protective to a fault, but she had detected no other brotherly offenses in his behavior.

"Charles thinks I have no sense of propriety, which is the gravest injustice, as if I do not know exactly with whom I may correspond when he is nothing but a despicable...spy."

"A spy?"

"Yes, he's looked at my post. Oh, he denies it, but he accused me of writing to..." For a moment Octavia stared blankly at the cup and the pile of ginger crumbs. Then with a sigh she continued. "To a young man in the most indiscreet way, when I have only written very proper notes to you and to the dear marchioness."

"I see," said Harriet. She felt the violation of it, the injury and hurt of a beloved brother's lack of trust when Octavia felt herself blameless. She, too, had accused Wynford of spying when he followed them to the Burlington Arcade, but the word, with its implication of secret intentions, was wrong. She tried to turn Octavia's thoughts in a happier direction. "I'm sorry to hear that things are in such a sad way between you, just when he is to take you to Lady Hardwicke's ball."

"Well, I should forgive him, I know, but how can I when he has not an ounce of respect for my understanding or my ability to manage my own life?"

"How did he come to misjudge you so?" Harriet asked. There must be another side to the story. She guessed that a shift had taken place in Octavia's feelings, a shift that the girl was just beginning to understand. She had come to London suffering from the hurt inflicted by the unnamed young man, but now it was Wynford who wounded her.

Octavia remained silent, looking down at the crumbled ginger cake. "I suppose he can't help it, you know. He can't forget saving me as a babe under those stupid fishing nets."

"The old history? Do you want to tell me about it?" Harriet invited.

Octavia's eyes took on a faraway look. Then she squared her shoulders and lifted her chin. "Yes."

"When Charles was eleven, I think, and I one, our mother took us with her to France to her grandfather's vineyards near the town of Saumur. I don't know why she did it. It was not a good time to be English and traveling in France, but our mother could always pass for French. Charles has told me that she passed for the wife of a country merchant. We were to stay for the summer, but we had not been long in the country when something happened in Paris, and we had to leave at once, traveling fast, only in the early hours and at dusk.

"We were to cross the Channel in a fishing boat from a beach near Dieppe, but there was a storm, and the boat didn't come. We waited a day or so more—I don't know how long, but Mama took us to the beach to play late one afternoon with the clouds clearing, and that's when the soldiers found us. Mama had a glass to look for the fishing boat. She saw the soldiers first and made Charles take me away. He was supposed to leave the beach, but he could not move quickly carrying me, so he burrowed in the sand under some fishing nets left there to dry."

Octavia paused. Harriet held her breath, suspended in the story. It was like the moment of being tossed from a horse. One hung briefly in the air, powerless to undo one's error, as the ground rushed up.

Octavia drew a shaky breath, and plunged on.

"Charles pressed his thumb to my lips to keep me from crying out. I bit him, and he still bears the scar, but they did not find us. The soldiers killed our mother while we hid. Charles did not hear her cry out. He waited a long time, hoping, I think, that she would call to us. Once it grew dark, he got us to the meeting place. He had some crumbly cheese in his pocket, which he gave me to eat. In the night the Englishmen came, and Charles told them what he feared. They found our mother's body farther down the beach and took us all back to England. My brother had to tell the story over and over again to someone in the government, but it was years before he told me what had happened."

Harriet held herself steady, her hands around the fragile cup. For all of Octavia's composure in the telling, it was a tale at odds with a room full of comforts. Warring impulses coursed through her. She wanted to embrace the girl. She wanted to apologize to Wynford for thinking him excessive in his concern for his sister's safety. And she wanted to know the truth. Certain particulars of the story struck her as having great significance—the clandestine nature of the visit, the mysterious event in Paris, the delayed fishing boat, the telling of the tale to someone in government. Above all, she thought, a boy who had seen and felt what Wynford had seen and felt might become a most fierce protector of his sister.

"You must wonder at my story, Miss Swanley," Octavia said. "Papa told me long ago that I must be very careful with such a history. He did not want anyone to pity me, you see, or to think badly of Mama for taking us to France. It all happened so long ago."

"Thank you for telling me, Octavia." Her throat ached, but she kept her voice as level as she could. "We will say no more about it, if you wish, but I think you may be right about your brother."

"About my brother?"

"Yes," Harriet said. "He was just Jasper's age when it all happened, wasn't he?"

"Jasper's age? Oh." Octavia paused. A look of rueful comprehension came into her eyes. "I never think of him as young, but he must have been."

"He was," Harriet said. She had utterly misjudged him, never imagining that the memory of such horror lurked under the smooth air and manner of a London gentleman. "He can't forget holding you under those fishing nets can he?"

"I suppose he can't." Octavia acknowledged. She sighed. "But how can I get him to see that I'm no longer a babe?"

* * * *

Goldsworthy liked Charles's new line of inquiry. They sat in the gloom of his office on the dark afternoon as the snow began to descend. Wilde had left coffee and some sweet, honey-coated pastries on the big desk.

"That's the ticket, lad," Goldsworthy said. "Spies are never disinterested parties. They are men—"

Charles raised a brow.

"—or women, who have known...betrayal." Goldsworthy's eyes darted back and forth as his mind worked. "They've learned to distrust appearances."

Charles drank his coffee and waited. Though it was rare for Goldsworthy to share his thinking, there was more coming. Lynley had told him that Goldsworthy had been in the spy business for over twenty years. The man was ancient and ageless at once like a mighty oak with a gnarled trunk and a green head.

"She avoids being in company with Wellington, does she?" Goldsworthy prompted.

"She does, though he's the man more than any other who could help a royalist widow establish her claim to property in France." Charles had now seen her turn away from the duke three times.

Goldsworthy chuckled. "And our duke has always had an eye for the ladies. Her avoiding him rather confirms your suspicion that she was in Paris during the occupation. So who else might have noticed her? How old would she have been?"

"Twenty-three, perhaps. No more than twenty-five," Charles said.

Goldsworthy's lively eyes did their thinking dance. "If the marchioness was in Paris during the occupation, she could have caught some Englishman's eye, and if his intentions were less than honorable, if she suffered at his hands, she might be susceptible to Zovsky's recruiting methods."

Charles had considered the possibility and its limits. He and Perry now had intelligence reports of various parties and balls at which the English officers and their Russian counterparts had mingled in that time of reveling in the allies' victory and the delights of the great city suddenly reopened to them. If they were right, somewhere in the mass of gossip and detail would be the story of a scandal, of a dashing officer who pursued a young Russian woman and broke her heart or, worse, ruined her.

"The theory is not without its limits," Charles admitted. "Even if such an event is part of the marchioness's history, the man who wronged her would have to be dead now for her to move so openly about London."

Goldsworthy shook his great head. "She's a bold one. You've seen yourself that she goes everywhere even though she must avoid Wellington."

Charles nodded and shifted the conversation back to the most important point. "Betrayal may be her motive, sir, but what we don't know is her mission." Charles could make no sense of it so far. "She takes little interest in men with obvious government ties, except for Edenhorn. She is remarkably open in her movements. She takes pains to let me know where she is going and with whom. One sees her daily in public places. One could almost suppose her innocent except that she tries so hard."

"Raises your suspicions, doesn't it?" The big man chuckled.

It did. From the beginning he'd doubted the marchioness's authenticity. Her willingness to provide a family tree, her open references to the vineyards of Saumur and the members of his family, her persistent presence wherever Charles went... Perry had discovered with Faraday's help that some of the ink on the family tree was quite recent, no more than a few months old. Great Uncle Victor was a fabrication.

* * * *

Harriet spent hours pondering Octavia's revelations, unable to stop thinking about Wynford, the man who wanted to dance with her. Her contrary impressions of him had undergone two complete reversals in an hour. As the spy who read Octavia's post, he appeared nearly as overbearing and blind to his sister's happiness as Harriet's own brother had once been. As the boy under the fishing nets, she thought he might be forgiven almost anything in his desire to protect his sister from harm.

Harriet wandered the house, absently collecting items from Lady Luxborough's list that were meant to go into the country the following week with the remaining servants. Unaccountably, among them was the sheet music for the old carol, "The Holly and the Ivy," which Pris had been practicing for weeks. Harriet discovered the music under an embroidery frame left on a chair in the second-best drawing room.

When she picked it up, she read the words of the old song to push Wynford from her mind. "The holly bears a berry as red as any blood. The holly bears a prickle as sharp as any thorn. The holly bears a bark as bitter as any gall." Then she laughed at her quick descent into melancholy, knowing that Pris laboring at her instrument was not the least bit likely to inspire melancholy in anyone but her music master.

Instantly her thoughts returned to Wynford. Octavia's revelation of the family history was at odds with Wynford's usual composure and his untroubled manner as a single gentleman with a flirtatious smile.

Harriet did not quite understand how the boy on the beach and the man who teased her for a dance could be the same person. Snatches of conversation between them would come to mind to make her stop in the middle of a room. Then she would pick up Lady Luxborough's list again and return to work.

There was more to the story than the horror Wynford had faced as a boy. By Octavia's own admission, she had related a secondhand account. The girl had not questioned elements of the tale that struck Harriet as pointing to quite another explanation for Lady Wynford's death on that beach.

It was nearly four, quite dark, and snowing steadily when Harriet at last placed Lady Luxborough's full workbasket on the demilune table in the front hall. At that moment Cat's distinctive howl came from the back of the stairs behind the door to the yellow room. When she opened it, he exploded into the hall, ran circles around her, and skidded to a stop at the front door, regarding her expectantly. Her thoughts immediately underwent another revolution. Her position in the world was clear. She was not an eligible young miss to spend an afternoon wholly absorbed in thinking about a man like Wynford. She was a doer-of-favors, a collector of odds and ends, a dog-minder, an afterthought, as easily left behind as Cat.

"Oh dear." She laughed at him. "They've probably not missed you yet, and it will be too late to turn back." He danced a bit at the door. "I'll get my cloak," she said. "But you'll have to wait for morning for a proper walk."

The husband hunter must not form her opinion of a gentleman's character solely upon the foundation of his present actions and manner in society. Every man has a past. What she has heard of him from others must be tested with careful observation and a willingness to listen for that history of his actions and relations which sheds the truest light upon his character.

—*The Husband Hunter's Guide to London*

Chapter 17

In the morning Harriet took the dog out before breakfast. She woke early from a fitful sleep with the same questions disturbing her peace. She supposed it was always so when the family was away. She might not truly be one of them, but their presence was a comfort. She had not considered that her place with them would ever end, but now she could see that the end had always been there.

To dance or not to dance. That was the question. Harriet had already weakened her position by agreeing to go to the Hardwicke ball. Yesterday Lady Luxborough had advised Harriet with her characteristic frankness to take advantage of Wynford's interest and return to society. Harriet knew that if she chose to dance, she would be leaving the sanctuary she had found with the Luxboroughs. She would be exposed to censure and condemned for putting herself forward and seeking a match far above her deserts.

A fresh layer of snow covered the iron railings along Mount Street and made the flagstones treacherous. Harriet concentrated on her footing, heedless of where she and Cat were headed. They soon reached the park, and she let Cat off his lead. The sky was still heavy with more snow to come, and the great expanse looked as if an army of Gunter's cake icers had worked through the night, touching every branch and blade with white. Cat bounded over the icy grass to greet his bird friends with deep barks, sending flocks of blackbirds and robins into sudden squawking flight. He tried with more stealth to make himself agreeable to a pair of wood ducks in the reeds at the edge of the lake, but they, too, were having none of his overtures.

Watching him lifted Harriet's spirits. Whatever she decided, she had enjoyed a remarkable degree of freedom in her position. She had chosen her life and had not thought any man could tempt her to go back on that choice. But Wynford, with his desire to dance with her and the sprig of mistletoe in his pocket, had put an end to her perfect contentment with those old choices. With her new knowledge of his past, he had stirred her compassion.

She had come to no resolution about whether to dance or not to dance when her teeth began to chatter. She summoned Cat and left the park. From Curzon Street, she turned up South Audley heading home. Cat no longer tugged at his lead but rather ambled along, stopping every few feet to investigate a new scent. The lead was slack in Harriet's hand, and she was admiring the rosy tint on the low clouds overhead, when the dog darted down the narrow Lansdowne passage that wound its way through Mayfair, the lead flopping in his wake. She called, but to no avail. Some powerful scent had caught him, and he was not to be deterred from the pursuit. He skidded on the ice as he negotiated the turn onto Hay Street and disappeared. Harriet moved as quickly as she could over the icy stones.

His tail flashed around the corner of Dover Street, and when she reached the spot, she saw him bound up the front steps of a gray stone townhouse in the middle of the block. She recognized the house at once and hurried on, anticipating the dog's inevitable outcry. Before she could reach him, he began to howl with the deep-voiced baying peculiar to his mix of English and French hound.

At that hour in the snowy street there was no covering sound of traffic. The penetrating howl could be heard by all the sleepers on the block. Windows, velvet curtains, and damask bed hangings would not stop that wail. A little breathless, Harriet reached the steps where Cat had taken his stand. She seized the dog's lead and bent down to put an arm around his chest.

"Cat, it's too early. No one can come out to play yet," she said. She tugged on the lead, but Cat lifted his nose and raised another howl, his hindquarters firmly planted on the doorstep.

Across the street a door opened, and a surly voice shouted, "Muzzle that dog, wench, or I'll muzzle 'im for ye," while footsteps sounded in the house. Harriet dropped to her knees to hold Cat as the door opened by some invisible hand, and there in the entry stood Wynford, a dark blue dressing gown over his shirt and trousers, his feet in slippers. Harriet had been thinking for hours of the boy on the beach with a babe in his arms. Her mind shifted once again to take in Wynford the man. He was as striking as he had been the morning he'd come to ask a favor of her, tall, well-made, with an easy grace of posture.

Their eyes met and held, and Harriet watched as the memory of their first meeting surfaced in his gaze.

On that other December morning, she had been kneeling with her arms around a dog outside the door to the tenants' hall of Dunraven Park. Wynford had come striding down the servants' passage, out of place in his elegance. He had been looking for someone to help him find a remedy for his ailing valet.

Now he raised one dark brow. Cat burst from her hold and shot into the marble entry, skidding to a stop at Wynford's feet.

"So Cat got left behind." He spoke, and Cat subsided at once, pressing his wet, muddy belly against the tiles and wagging his tail enthusiastically.

Wynford's gaze, piercing now, returned to her. "You were the girl that morning with the dog."

"My spaniel Nelson," she said, coming to her feet.

"You let me think you were a servant. Why?"

"You were very fine that morning." Harriet remembered him dressed all in brown for the shoot with gleaming boots that had not yet encountered mud. "I was in my oldest frock, muddied, my hair coming down, toweling off a wet dog." She had recognized him at once as one of her brother's prized guests, the ones she'd been warned to stay away from until presented in the drawing room. She had been conscious of Wynford's air of sophistication. He had seemed years older than she, at ease in the world. She was sixteen and never at ease. His mistaking her for a servant, however, made her bold. She asked what brought him belowstairs. He'd apologized then for overstepping a guest's bounds and explained that he'd come in search of a draught or tisane, some remedy for his ailing valet.

She enlisted his aid to shut Nelson in the tenants' hall, explaining that the dog was apt to ruin the shoot if let loose, and led Wynford to the stillroom to find something for his man. It was there that she'd crossed the line, daring to be pert. She had some idea in her head that it would be a good jest to meet him later in the drawing room as her true self in her best dress and perhaps some of her mother's pearls.

But he had revealed that he was leaving within the hour. The disdain in the way he announced his intention had goaded her. "You don't wish to stay to meet the ladies of the house?" she had asked. "I doubt this house holds any true ladies," he said with such repugnance that a hot flood of shame had washed over her. It wasn't until it subsided that she'd realized she had no idea what prompted his contempt before they ever met. That evening her brother made it quite clear.

Ten years later with another unruly dog at her side she felt a rush of the old awkwardness. Then she had been playing a servant, now she was, if not a servant, nevertheless a woman sunk beneath his sphere. "I beg your pardon," she said. "I had no intention," she faltered. "Cat would not be dissuaded from coming here today."

"I see that," he said dryly.

"I did warn you not to pet him," she said, recovering her composure.

"And, of course, I did not listen. Will you have some coffee? To warm you? Perry's here." He stepped aside, letting Harriet see the open door to what appeared to be a library. Perry looked up from some papers on a table.

"Hello, Harry. Brought the dog, have you?" He turned back to the papers, tapping them with a finger. "Wynford, it's just as you suspected. There was a scandal involving an artillery major, named Ashton, and the daughter of a Russian general, Dimitri Dashkova. All covered up, of course. That girl could be our woman. The fellow's still alive, though."

Harriet directed her gaze away from Wynford. Beyond him was the lovely room with a Brussels carpet and leather-covered chairs. At Wynford's feet the muddy dog panted. She had set out with the firm intention of dismissing the man from her thoughts. Instead her wanderings had brought her to his door to be tempted by his beautiful...library.

"Thank you for the kind invitation. We won't interrupt your..." She wanted to call it work, for that's what it seemed to be. "Neither Cat nor I," she looked at her damp hem flecked with mud, "is in a fit state for a visit."

Wynford glanced at the dog. "What are the chances you can convince him to leave?"

He was maddeningly right. She had for years been the only person in the household outside of Jasper who could get Cat to obey voice commands. Now she had been replaced by a new idol. The awkwardness of her situation deepened.

"Perhaps..."

"Let me come with you. We should talk in any case." He shrugged out of his dressing gown. The careless gesture cast aside whatever he had been doing with Perry and claimed her whole attention.

"You will be safe with me in the street, you know. There's no mistletoe hanging from the lampposts."

Color rose hotly in her cheeks, as if there were any danger of a kiss from him now that he had remembered who she truly was. "Do you want to talk about your sister?"

He shot her a glance that saw through the evasion and turned to give a few quick orders to his servants. A coat, hat, and gloves appeared. He donned them and gave the dog a look. Cat rose obediently and trotted to the door. Wynford offered Harriet his arm, and they set off.

The street had begun to fill with people. Servants shoveled snow from walkways and rooftops. Rattling carts and smooth-rolling carriages carved a dark, wet path through the white center of the street. Cat danced and ran in circles, returning excitedly to Wynford.

"Did my sister tell you how I offended her?" he asked. She was grateful for his willingness to shift the conversation from their own history to a less unsettling topic.

"Apparently you 'spied' on her post," Harriet said.

There was a check in his stride at the word "spied." They went some ways in silence before he spoke again. "Have I blundered irretrievably with her?"

"Irretrievably? The brother who saved his sister's life on a beach in France?"

"She told you our history then." His gaze sobered.

"She did."

"And?" he asked. "Did my past actions earn me forgiveness in the present?"

"Understanding, perhaps, if not yet forgiveness." Harriet faced him directly. "It is I who must beg pardon of you for thinking you an unnecessarily protective brother. If the dangers of a London Season are not those of Bonaparte's France, your desire to protect Octavia from them is entirely reasonable."

"Dance with me," he said, a gleam of laughter lighting his eyes. "And anything may be forgiven."

"I thought we had an understanding on that point." He set her off-balance again. He could not wish to dance with her now that he remembered their first meeting.

"I have the full support of Lady Luxborough, you know."

Harriet did know. "Yes, and I'll thank you not to join forces with my employer against my peace of mind and strength of resolution."

"You won't discourage me by letting me know that I am a temptation," he said with a grin. "What did she say to make you laugh like that yesterday?"

"Oh," said Harriet. "It was her description of Lady Hardwicke as a woman with a secret ambition to run a theater, who considers her guests the cast of a three-act farce and arranges her parties to promote scenes of discord. Lady Luxborough said I could very much oblige her by providing Lady Hardwicke with the spectacle of a governess flouting convention."

"And are you game to do it?" he asked.

"If we are bargaining for a dance, I must state my conditions as well."

"Name them," he said.

"If you will be serious for a moment."

"I am likely to be all too serious about a dance with you."

They had reached Mount Street and were now only steps from Luxborough House. "Your sister's account puzzles me. She necessarily relies on others for the story and accepts it with all its improbable details."

"You think it improbable that a band of rogue soldiers killed a defenseless woman?" He did not meet her gaze.

"I doubt they were rogue soldiers. Your sister does not know what the simple story reveals, and that's why you discourage her from telling it. Your mother, it appears, went to France on a mission of some sort, for our government, but apparently the participants were betrayed by someone in Paris." Harriet watched his stern profile. "She fled with her children to the rendezvous, but the storm delayed the boat from England and gave those who searched for her time to find her on that beach. With extraordinary presence of mind, she led them away from her children."

He stopped walking and stood looking down at the snow before Luxborough House with bleak, unseeing eyes. "It was a royalist plot to assassinate Bonaparte after the attempt in '04 failed. The conspirators had the support of our government and sent messages to one another through my mother in Saumur."

She had not expected the admission. She closed her hands into fists to refrain from reaching out to him. The dog, returning from a brief foray to the other side of the street with a stick in his mouth, had no such scruples and nudged Wynford's hand, bringing him back to the present. He turned to Harriet.

"You owe me a dance," he said, in a maddeningly imperturbable voice. "And I'll take nothing less than a waltz."

She nodded, expecting him to stop there.

"Since I am admitting things," he said with a dry laugh. "The post I saw belonged to the marchioness. Among her letters was one addressed to our neighbor Horace Gresham in a hand so like Octavia's that I had to ask her about it."

Instantly an image of Wynford's hard male presence in the blue silk dressing gown passed through Harriet's mind. For him to see the marchioness's post suggested a degree of intimacy between them that Harriet had not imagined, though his expression betrayed no shame or embarrassment in the admission.

"You did not tell Octavia where you saw the letter?" she asked in a faint voice.

"I did not, and she denies any improper correspondence." He laughed. "Octavia would find it strange, I know, but the thought of her writing to

Gresham, however indiscreet such a letter would be, troubles me less than the degree of trust she places in our...cousin."

Harriet noted the hesitation. "You do not believe the marchioness is your cousin."

He offered her a wry smile. "I doubt she is French at all."

"Of course." In Harriet's mind the details of the past and present continued to rearrange themselves. "The marchioness did not know Marie Rambert's name or reputation, did not understand the insult she had offered the woman."

"Yes, I noticed that. It is one of many inconsistencies in her story."

"Then who and why..." Harriet broke off, realizing that she was far from understanding his interest in the marchioness or the woman's particular attentions to Octavia. But it involved Perry, and she tried to recall what she had just heard about some Russian general's daughter.

Wynford withdrew into his thoughts and absently tossed the dog's stick in a high arc over the street. Cat gave chase and returned obediently to drop the stick at his idol's feet. When Wynford looked up, she thought him about to ask her something, but he simply rang the bell. "Safely delivered to your door. We have a bargain then for Lady Hardwicke's ball."

She nodded.

A footman opened the door, and Wynford ordered Cat inside, bowed, and turned away. She watched him, contradictory ideas jostling one another in her head. He was three houses down the street when she cried, "Wait."

With no regard for her footing, she ran to him.

He caught her gloved hands in his, his grip tight, and steadied her, an amused look in his eyes. "What is it?" he asked.

"You must believe Octavia," she said. "She told me that since she has been in London she has written only to me and to the marchioness. Don't you see? That means the marchioness has in her possession, as I have in mine, samples of your sister's handwriting."

His expression changed. "You're suggesting forgery? The marchioness writing to Gresham in my sister's hand?"

"Yes," she said a little breathlessly. "Octavia would never write to Gresham. The things she's said to me make it plain that Gresham has transferred his affections to another woman—recently, abruptly."

"She told you this?" he asked.

"Hints only, but the loss of his regard would explain her desire to make herself into a different girl and win a husband by Christmas. What doesn't make sense, I suppose, is what the marchioness is about writing a letter to Gresham in your sister's hand."

A look of menacing grimness hardened his features. "Indeed," he said. "The marchioness's motives are hard to fathom."

He seemed to remember then that he held her hands in the public street. Heads of passersby turned. "Thank you," he said, "for teaching me to do justice to my sister."

"She is perhaps stronger than you think and more like you than you suppose."

His look changed again, all harshness gone. "I must ask," he said.

She lowered her gaze from his piercing one.

"What happened after I left your brother's house that day?"

She lifted her chin and met his searching gaze with as steady a look as she could manage. "I found I could not marry the man my brother chose for me."

* * * *

Perry paced the library when Wynford returned. "It's no good," Perry said, looking downcast. "All the gossip points to Major Ashton, a rakehell in his day, but the fellow's alive, and as apt to stroll up Bond Street or show his face in a card room as you or I. In fact, I'm sure I saw him last week in the park on a bay hack with Sommersby."

"And the general's daughter?" Charles asked.

"Daughters," said Perry. "Irina and Sophia."

"Do we know which one caught the major's eye? Are they both living? Married?" asked Charles.

Perry, who never forgot a bit of scandal, grinned at him. "Brilliant." He went back to the notes on the desk. "The major pursues one of the girls, perhaps to her ruin..."

"Oh," said Charles, "almost surely to her ruin."

"And perhaps there is no redress. The English close ranks and protect the young officer from the consequences of his vile behavior, so the sister has reason to hate not only the man, but the nation."

Charles nodded. He didn't like it, but it looked to him as if the ruin of his own sister was at the heart of the marchioness's scheme.

"A little more digging," said Perry, "and we'll know whether our marchioness is Sophia or Irina." He went back to his papers.

"Perry, to whom did Dunraven want to marry his sister?"

"The man she refused, you mean?"

Charles nodded.

"Torrington, I think."

The misery of a ball gone wrong is the more acute for the expectation of pleasure that preceded it.

—The Husband Hunter's Guide to London

Chapter 18

Until Harriet stood on the threshold of Lady Hardwicke's ballroom and heard her old name announced, she did not fully realize the folly of saying yes to Wynford. She had told herself she would dance the two dances permitted and that in such a crowd at such a gathering no one would remark on the minor impropriety of a governess waltzing with a viscount. She had further convinced herself that a little vigilance on her part was all that was needed to protect Octavia from the missteps a girl might make at her first grand ball. She saw instantly that she was wrong on both counts.

At the decidedly spinsterish age of twenty-six, this was her first ball as much as it was Octavia's. Lady Luxborough, in deference to Harriet's scruples, had never asked her to attend a ball with Anne or Camille. Harriet's knowledge of dancing came from serving as partner to each of her charges as they learned their steps, or playing for all of them at impromptu dance parties in the country. Now she saw she was as green as Octavia, as susceptible to the excitement and wretchedness a ball could produce.

And this was not any ball. Lady Hardwicke's theatrical disposition was apparent at once. The ballroom was a play of light and dark with bright pools under the great chandeliers and shadowy recesses along the walls and under the great gallery for clandestine meetings. At each open door on the terrace side of the room stood small green groves of potted yew and fir trees scenting the air and beckoning guests to escape constraint in the darkness beyond. Enough mistletoe and holly hung from the chandeliers and wall sconces to satisfy a horde of ancient Druids gathered to celebrate the solstice. A dozen musicians played from a dais at one end of the grand room. Guests leaned together on benches in the shadows under the open gallery above. Ladies' fans fluttered in a heated atmosphere of restless extravagance. Gowns were cut low, laughter was raucous, and champagne flowed. Proper conduct hadn't a prayer. She clung to the arm Wynford offered her as they stood waiting to enter, and he leaned down to say in her ear, his breath disturbing her curls, "I see that I didn't need to bring my mistletoe."

A shiver went down her spine, and they stepped into the ballroom.

They stood just long enough for Harriet to lament her lack of acquaintance among Lady Hardwicke's guests when the marchioness approached. In a dark green gown, the woman looked as if she had emerged from one of the groves of potted trees. Accompanying her was a young man in a scarlet-and-gold regimental jacket. Introductions were made.

Captain Fanshaw had the confident air of a man aware of his personal advantages: height, broad shoulders, abundant golden hair, and pleasing symmetry of his features marred only by a slight bruising on one cheek near his nose. Octavia beamed her entire satisfaction at his handsome appearance, while at Harriet's side Wynford stood in frowning silence.

"Oh dear," the marchioness said, casting a wry glance at Wynford's waistcoat. "Purple?"

"Heliotrope," replied Wynford with a smile that did not reach his eyes.

The marchioness raised a brow. "Octavia, you'd best keep apart from your brother lest he ruin the effect of your gown."

"I doubt anyone will notice Wynford's waistcoat," said Fanshaw, "when he may look upon Miss Davenham's dress." He offered her a besotted gaze as if no one else existed.

Octavia cast him a doubting look in return. "Dear marchioness," she said, "I trust you and Lady Harriet to keep my brother company."

An expression of disdain crossed the marchioness's face at the use of Harriet's title, and the conversation grew awkward, as Captain Fanshaw offered Octavia compliments and Octavia tried to deflect his flattery. He seemed to have a low estimate of female intelligence, and at last Octavia simply suggested that they dance.

Their movement broke up the small party, as Harriet knew it must. Wynford, in his heliotrope waistcoat, turned to follow the marchioness. Harriet turned to find a place near Lady Hardwicke when her hand was seized and Wynford whispered, "Do not forget. You owe me a waltz."

* * * *

Harriet did not know how the time passed until Wynford came for her. He bowed and led her into the circle of dancers forming in the center of the room. Harriet's drawing room dances with her charges as they learned their steps had not prepared her for placing her left hand on Wynford's right arm and feeling his arm slide around her. With each touch she yielded her arms, her waist, her hands. She could not deny the energy that passed between them as their gloved palms met, closing them in position, her skirts swishing up against his trousers like the foam of a wave touching a shore. The musicians took preliminary passes at their strings, and there seemed to be no way to hold her head that did not invite intimacy, Wynford looking down into her eyes, his mouth inches from her lips, his breath against her curls.

He raised his left brow in the tiniest question. She realized that his face, so often controlled, was open to her in its smallest changes.

"What?" he asked.

"I was merely thinking about Faraday and electromagnetism." She would think of science and steady her racing pulse. In her head she could see a diagram of Faraday's theory of the flow of energy between magnets.

"Are we poles that repel or attract?" he asked.

She laughed. "I am being foolish about this, aren't I? Agreeing to dance with you is...a mere nothing, isn't it?"

"Oh, I don't think so," he said. "I think it's everything."

Then the music started. Her grip tightened on his arm as he sent her back into the dipping motion of the dance. Up they came, turning, moving together. With a hand at her waist he assumed control, sending them into a world apart, governed by the music until the room around them disappeared in a whirling blur and there was only Wynford. She smiled and laughed up at him with a kind of freedom she had never known.

As the dance came to an end, he whirled her into a corner of the ballroom where the candles in the sconces had not been lit. The music stopped. He did not release her, but pulled her close against him in the dark. Her head rested on his chest. His heart beat under her ear.

They stood that way until a wry laugh shook him, as if there were some joke. "Will you marry me, Harry?" he asked.

She pulled back in his arms and lifted her gaze to his, ready to question his sanity, but he laid a finger on her lips.

"Does it seem mad to you? A man in a purple waistcoat asking for your hand? Then don't answer yet," he said solemnly. He reached up and broke off a sprig of mistletoe hanging from the darkened wall sconce. "If you find that you can say yes, wear this in your hair."

He handed her the sprig and leaned down to kiss her, their lips meeting in the lightest touch that changed instantly to a desperate clinging of mouths. He pulled her closer against his sinewy length. Her hands slid around his shoulders, reaching up to hold his head to hers. Her body strained against the barriers of linen, silk, and whalebone, the lightest and most absolute of barriers, like propriety itself. Her heart began a glad hammering. Shooting stars of sensation went streaking through her, and she was lost in the kiss, falling upward into the depths of the night sky, when she thought she heard a voice calling from a great distance.

"Wynford."

She pulled back in his arms.

"Perry?" Wynford replied, his gaze still on Harriet, his hand firm on her back.

"Thank God I found you. No time to lose," said Perry. He halted in front of them, his gaze going from one to the other. "Oh, hello, Harry. Sorry to intrude. Wynford proposing, is he? Matter of national importance. Need to borrow Wynford for a moment."

"What is it?" Wynford asked.

"It's Ashton. He's in the card room. We must get to him before the marchioness does."

"Coming, Perry."

Wynford turned to Harriet, his face masked to her now, his thoughts elsewhere. "Find Octavia," he said. "Stay with her."

"Of course," she said, a woman of sense and steadiness returning to herself from the madness of the moment.

* * * *

Perry led Charles to a card room where gentlemen not inclined to dance had gathered around five green baize tables intent on various forms of play. Ashton, in black evening clothes, lounged back in his chair, a glass of claret in hand, apparently bored with the play at his table. He was well past forty, but his hair remained thick and dark. From the straining of his white damask waistcoat over his middle and the blurring of the features of his once-handsome face, he appeared to be a man given to indulgence. The folds of his chin met the folds of his neckcloth.

Perry stepped up behind him and spoke a discreet word in his ear.

The man looked up under heavy lids, his gaze catching Charles standing opposite.

"May we have a word?" Charles asked.

Ashton threw his cards on the table. "I'm out, gentlemen," he told his friends. He drew himself to his feet and followed Perry to a sideboard laden with glasses and decanters of spirits.

"What's this about?" he asked Charles, filling his glass.

"Ten years ago in Paris there was a scandal—"

"I say," protested Ashton, stiffening. "Ancient history. You can't bring Paris up against a fellow now, besides—" He fell silent, looking aggrieved.

Charles began again. Ashton had slipped. He made no denial. "Besides what?"

"Who are you? How do you know about Paris? It was all concealed."

"Never mind who we are."

Ashton's eyes narrowed, almost disappearing in his puffy face. "Hah! You're government, aren't you? Sent to plague a man. Listen, I'm an old married man now. What's past is past."

"You think that if it comforts you, Ashton," Charles said. "Besides what?"

"The girl was willing, you know. Her damned Cossack father was the problem. Sent her into a decline, or she became ill. I don't know. I told you, ancient history."

"And the father came after you?" Charles would have gone after him, after any man who carelessly ruined a girl.

Ashton shook his head. "Not the father, the sister. She was a madwoman. She tried to shoot me at the Hotel Breteuil on the Rue de Rivoli." He spoke like a man offended by a breach of good manners.

"The sister?"

"Sophia, the mad one." He shuddered. "Irina died."

Charles might not know the full story, but he had heard enough to understand Sophia Dashkova's resentment against Ashton and perhaps against England. "Are you armed, Ashton?"

"Armed?"

"Yes. You'll be interested to know that Sophia is here tonight."

Ashton's pasty face blanched. "Here?" His gaze darted for the door. He looked around for somewhere to put his glass.

"Does she know about me? Does she know I'm here?"

"It would not surprise me in the least, Major," Charles said, and he knew it was true. Whatever her mission was, Sophia Dashkova was ready to make her move.

"Gentlemen, you must excuse me," Ashton announced.

"Very wise, Ashton. I'd leave at once, if I were you."

As Ashton hurried off, Charles and Perry turned back toward the ballroom. Charles's mind ranged over the danger. The marchioness, or Dashkova as he must now think of her, had bided her time, appearing harmless, making arrangements, and now he had no doubt she would act.

"Perry, I've got to find Octavia. Can you find that footman of mine, Wilde?"

"The fellow whose ears stick out?"

"Yes. He should be near the cloakroom. I need him to take an urgent message."

"Will you unmask the marchioness here?" Perry asked.

"I have to find Octavia first," Charles replied grimly. And Harriet. He had no doubt that Harriet would protect his sister from anyone who offered Octavia harm.

They parted at the stairs, Perry hurrying downward, Charles turning back to the ballroom.

* * * *

While Harriet clutched her sprig of mistletoe, Octavia danced a quadrille with a raffish officer friend of Captain Fanshaw's who hardly looked at her. Fanshaw, after his early attentions to Octavia, had disappeared. Harriet gathered that the girl had discouraged his heavy-handed flattery. The marchioness was nowhere to be seen. Somehow in Lady Hardwicke's wooded ballroom everything had become confused. Octavia, who desperately wanted a husband, had no prospects. Harriet, who had never dreamed of a proposal, had a husband if she wanted him.

Standing absently at the edge of the dance, she kept her gaze on Octavia, but she could think only of Wynford. He was not who he appeared to be—the idle, foppish man of fashion with a taste for colorful waistcoats. He was a man on a government mission. His sister had called him a spy for looking at her post, but it occurred to Harriet that he might, in fact, be another sort of spy, and not the man she thought she knew at all. He had not intended his proposal. He was careful, but he was also dangerous. His mind was on the marchioness—and even Octavia, the sister he meant to protect, had been forgotten in the spy business that consumed him.

The moment the thought occurred, someone trod on Harriet's skirts. She glanced down at her rolled satin hem drooping on the floor and gathered a fistful of fabric in one gloved hand. Looking up again, she saw Octavia, white-faced and rigid with emotion, embroiled in a conversation in the center of the room, attracting the attention of dancers who had perforce to navigate around her and the couple with whom she spoke. Her partner had apparently abandoned her.

The couple were a young gentleman in black and his tall, elegant-looking partner glittering in a champagne silk gown with gold braid trim, a triple strand of pearls looped around her neck, and a white ostrich feather curling down around fair golden curls and haughty face. Harriet clutched her skirts and her mistletoe and picked her way to them through the movement of the dance.

"You," she heard Octavia say. "Why are you here?"

"You invited me, you ninny," answered the young man.

"Invited you?"

"In your letter a sennight ago, as Miss Burrell can confirm." He smiled at his companion.

"You had a letter from me?" Octavia demanded. "And you showed it to her? You must be mad."

"Well, I'm not mad. As my fiancée, Miss Burrell shares all my concerns. You are the one behaving like a hoyden, boasting of your conquests in London and daring me to show my face here."

Octavia's face went a shade whiter.

Harriet broke in. "I beg your pardon, mister...? Might we take this conversation where we do not have to share it with the whole room?"

The young man turned on her. "I'm Gresham. Who are you?" he demanded.

Harriet drew herself up. "Lady Harriet Swanley," she said quietly. "Miss Davenham is with me and her brother this evening. Again, may I suggest that we take our conversation off the dance floor?"

Something in Harriet's voice or manner made Gresham swallow whatever intemperate remark he had been about to make.

"Come, Caroline," he said to his companion, turning his back on Octavia.

Harriet put herself between Octavia and the many pairs of eyes watching them, and the group reassembled at the side of the room under one of the mistletoe-bedecked wall sconces. They stood a little sheltered from the crowd's notice by a stand of yew and fir. A breath of icy air from an open terrace door swirled around their ankles.

Gresham and Octavia glared at each other, but Harriet gave the edge to Gresham. He had his fiancée's hand tucked protectively in the crook of his arm. If Octavia had been capable of laughing at his stance of outraged male dignity, she could regain the advantage, but Octavia looked close to tears.

"Horace Gresham," she said in a quavering voice. "I never wrote to you. Whatever your opinion of me, I have done nothing improper. Furthermore, as Lady Harriet can tell you, I have been so wholly engaged at balls and parties and lectures and the theater, that I have had no time to think of... old childhood friends. You are mistaken."

"Mistaken? Don't I know your hand? Didn't we take lessons together from the vicar? And don't I know you? You ride neck or nothing, you skate like a boy, and you're capable of freaks and starts, like haring off to

London on the stage with that silly book my mother gave you. Next thing I know, you write me that you have a husband in your pocket and dare me to come and see him. Well, I'm here. Where's this husband you've bagged?"

The question, delivered as a taunt, seemed to strike Octavia as a blow, but she squared her shoulders and lifted her chin. "You gave me that book. It's not silly, and I never, never wrote to you. You don't know me at all."

"But there's no husband, is there? Hah," he said.

For a moment Octavia appeared to hold her ground. Then tears welled up, and she broke and ran stumbling out onto the dance floor. Checked by the whirl of dancers, she turned and slipped into the artificial grove that led to the terrace. Harriet ached for her. Across the room, leaning down from the upper gallery, was the marchioness, her icy gaze observing them closely.

"I knew it was a fool's errand to come here tonight," said Gresham.

Harriet felt a strong desire to take him by his fashionable lapels and shake him, but she merely said, "You're wrong, you know, Mr. Gresham. Octavia never wrote you that letter. You've been duped."

"By whom?" he asked.

"It doesn't matter. What did the letter say?"

As Gresham began to explain, Harriet saw Captain Fanshaw pass through the terrace doors. She cut off Gresham's explanation and hurried after Octavia. The girl would be at her most vulnerable, and Harriet had no doubt that the marchioness wanted it that way.

As she stepped into the little grove at the entrance to the terrace, cold air hit her and she stumbled over her torn hem. A hand gripped her arm, jerking her back into the ballroom.

"Where are you off to?" snarled a voice.

Steadying herself, she turned to meet her brother's gaze. "Where I go is none of your concern, Lionel."

He glared at her, but she stared him down until he dropped her hand. They had not spoken in ten years. His face, in feature so like her own, shocked her. It was diffused with dull anger, the dark brows lowered, the mouth cruel and sullen, the gray eyes unsmiling.

"What do you think you are doing here?" he asked. "You have no right to bring yourself to the notice of the fashionable world."

"Is that what you imagine I was doing?"

"What else? Need a husband? Tired of feeding at the Luxborough trough?"

Harriet refused to rise to the attempt to goad her. Octavia was out on the terrace, where Captain Fanshaw would surely find her. "Excuse me, Lionel."

"No." He shook his head. "You'll hear me out. You ruined your chances in the world long ago when you refused to do your duty to obey your brother and marry advantageously for your family's sake."

"It was never my duty to marry a cruel and unprincipled man."

"Don't think you can have Wynford now. He turned you down flat. He left that shooting party without even taking a look. You've been sunk for so long, you have no idea how odd an appearance you make."

"How I appear doesn't matter to you, Lionel. You washed your hands of me long ago. Now, I have a duty to perform." She turned and stepped out onto the terrace.

She shivered with the cold, standing for a moment, letting her eyes adjust to the dark. Then she gripped her torn skirts firmly in one fist and began her search. Torches flared from several brackets along the wall, giving a dim light. The cold seemed to have discouraged all but the most amorous, or perhaps the most drunken, of Lady Hardwicke's guests from lingering. Those who did clung to one another. But she saw no scarlet coat or poppy-colored gown.

Harriet stepped back inside the ballroom, hit at once by its warmth after the chill of the night. Another waltz was in progress, and, more anxious now, she began to work her way around the edge of the room toward the benches in the shadows under the gallery.

As she reached the darkened stretch, a man's foot sprawled in her path. She glanced at him to ask for help, but his eyes stared at her unseeing. His body listed to the right against a cushion.

A dreadful suspicion crossed her mind. She reached out to touch him. "Are you well, sir?" she asked.

At her touch, his shoulders slid sideways down the wall. His head hit the seat cushion, and a trickle of blood escaped his unmoving lips.

The rush of attentions from an insincere man is likely to be as heady as an ascent in a hot air balloon and equally likely to lead to a tumultuous descent.

—*The Husband Hunter's Guide to London*

Chapter 19

When Charles returned to the ballroom, the musicians had stopped playing for the supper interlude, and he perceived at once the difficulty of finding his sister and Miss Swanley in the sea of bobbing ostrich plumes as the crowd pressed toward Lady Hardwicke's supper room. He set himself to search the room, methodically slowing the sweep of his gaze. He made little progress before he was knocked roughly aside by a gentleman with a glass of claret in his hand.

The wine spilled, and the man swore viciously. He offered no apology but stared at Charles, shaking the drops of wine from his cuffs. "Wynford."

"Dunraven." Charles mustered what civility he could for Harriet Swanley's older brother, the Earl of Dunraven. When Charles had asked her to marry him, he'd forgotten his distaste for her brother. Dunraven's hair and eyes, even the shape of his face, proclaimed the relationship. Everything except the harsh, resentful spirit.

"You've got a nerve," Dunraven said.

"Have I?"

"Bringing my sister into fashionable society where she has no place."

"I beg your pardon. It's true. The company here is far beneath her. I mean to remove her from it as soon as I can. Have you seen her?"

Dunraven peered drunkenly at him as if Charles had made an obscure joke. "Hah! What do you know! Don't be fooled by that façade of the meek governess. She's a stubborn, strong-willed jade."

"Disobeyed you, did she? Refused Torrington's suit?" Charles continued to look for Octavia and Harriet.

"Damn fool, Torrington. If he hadn't shot the dog, he could have had her." Dunraven tossed back the last of the wine in his glass.

An icy chill settled in Charles's gut. He saw a kneeling girl with her arms around a dog, her gray eyes lifted to his. He kept his voice bland by a supreme effort. "He shot Nelson, her black spaniel?"

"Worthless animal deserved shooting. My foolish sister whistled away a fortune for a dog. But I made her pay," Dunraven said.

"Did you?" Charles asked. He could no longer keep the edge from his voice.

"What's it to you, Wynford? You could have had her if you'd stayed. You left." Dunraven shrugged.

"I found your method of getting a husband for your sister not to my taste."

"Like her method better? Try the terrace. She followed some officer out there."

The icy cold left him in a flash of anger that clenched his fists and flexed his arms and legs. He could lay Dunraven flat in an instant. In his mind he already stood over the man who had blighted Harriet's life.

Dunraven's eyes widened, and he backed away as he read Charles's intent. Before the bend and twist of Charles's body and upward arc of his fist could meet Dunraven's jaw, Charles caught himself and consciously opened his hands. He promised himself he would deal with Dunraven after he found Harriet and Octavia, and stepped out into the dark.

Within minutes he knew his search of the terrace was fruitless. Back in the heated ballroom, he turned away from the orchestra to circle the end of the ballroom for the benches under the gallery. There in the shadows sat Harriet Swanley, gently holding a dead man's hand in her lap.

"I thought you would find us," she said. "Who was he?"

"Ashton," he said, noting the trickle of blood on the man's chin.

"You think the marchioness did this?" she asked.

"Yes."

"She is not your cousin, is she?"

"No."

"How long have you known she was a fraud?"

"There was no proof until tonight. Ashton provided the proof."

"But you always believed she was dangerous?"

"Very."

"And yet you continued to let Octavia meet her?" She shuddered, a mix of bafflement and censure in her tone. She was in shock, but he could see that her orderly, unflinching mind kept working to make sense of what she saw.

How could he explain that the plan had been for Octavia to remain safe in the country? "I thought Octavia was in no danger while I had you," he said. It was true.

She nodded. "While you...did what...the government's work? It is spying, isn't it?" she asked. "That's what you're doing here tonight?"

"I am," he said grimly.

She nodded again. "And we, Octavia and I, we are part of your disguise? Like the waistcoats?"

"No."

She looked at him without reproach really, just an acknowledgment of a calculation he had not realized he'd made until now, the calculation that he could pursue and catch the marchioness without involving his sister or the woman he loved. He wondered if his mother had made a similar calculation that she could use her wits and skills to serve England without endangering her children.

"We have to find her, you know." She moved the dead man's hand to his lap, gently releasing it. "Gresham was here with his fiancée. He came because of a letter he received that he believed came from Octavia. He upset her. She ran out onto the terrace, observed by the marchioness. Captain Fanshaw followed."

"You'll help me?" he asked. He could not ask or expect it.

"Of course. We should speak with the footmen at the entry. There's a chance that Fanshaw has taken her somewhere."

Charles extended a hand to lift her from the bench. She rose. Charles stepped forward to set the dead man upright. Something brittle snapped under his boot, and he looked down to see a crushed sprig of mistletoe. He nudged it aside.

"I will send someone for Ashton," he said.

* * * *

In the hall at the foot of the grand staircase, Harriet and Wynford found a busy scene of leave-taking, with servants scurrying to do the bidding of numerous lofty and impatient persons. Wynford spoke with the man in charge of the cloakroom first and made sure that he understood he was to satisfy Harriet's questions. While Harriet conferred with him to secure their cloaks and hats, Wynford strode out into the cold to question the footmen and grooms attending to various vehicles in the lane.

As Harriet feared, the servant readily found her cloak and Wynford's greatcoat but not Octavia's. He admitted he had handed over Octavia's cloak earlier in the evening to a gentleman. He remembered because he had been rewarded with a gold coin.

"Was the man an officer?" Harriet asked. Sick dread filled her at the thought.

"Yes, miss," the footman answered.

"Did you see the girl?"

"No, miss."

Harriet thanked him and turned to find Wynford coming back to her. Her face must have betrayed her anxiety.

He seized her shoulders at once. "No luck?" he asked.

"A footman gave her cloak to an officer, but he didn't see her."

"I heard that Fanshaw left," he said. "More than thirty minutes ago. No markings on his coach."

"How do we pursue them?" she asked, handing Wynford his coat, hat, and gloves.

He took them from her with a faint smile, quickly donning his outerwear. "I pursue them. You go home and wait to hear from me."

"Do you think I can sit safe and idle at home not knowing where Octavia is? Knowing the marchioness may have her?"

"I can find you at Luxborough House more easily than I can find you here."

At that moment, a young man joined them. He had a handsome face; white, white teeth; and an air of brisk efficiency. "Sir," he said. "No sign of the marchioness or Captain Fanshaw."

"Lady Harriet," Wynford said, "this is Wilde. He will see you home." Wilde bowed.

"And Perry?" Wynford asked him.

Wilde shook his head. "Haven't seen him, sir."

Wynford took him aside, gave him instructions, and sent him off. Harriet slipped into her cloak, and when he turned back to her, he tied the strings under her chin. Their dance had been a brief moment out of time when she was not a governess and he was not a spy. When they separated, the moment would fade away, like a half-remembered tune one could faintly recall but not play again.

"You couldn't wear the mistletoe?" he asked.

She lifted her empty hand, realizing that she'd lost the little sprig somewhere in her pursuit of Octavia or discovery of the dead man. It had been the frailest of hopes, a bundle of brittle twigs, easily crushed.

"If you cannot leave the Luxboroughs for me," he said solemnly, "you must still leave them. You do not belong in yellow back rooms, in borrowed shawls..." He took her by the shoulders to draw her close.

She put up a hand, her palm flattening against the plane of his belly to hold him back, but her fingers closed around the silk of his waistcoat and clung. She leaned her head against his heart. His arms slipped around her. His chin rested on the top of her head.

"Your brother is wrong about you. You are above your company, not beneath it," he said. He lifted her face to his and kissed her, a kiss full of longing and regret.

He pulled back from their embrace. "I cannot tell you why the marchioness has come after us, but I will stop her. Wilde will see that you get home."

She nodded, swallowing a lump in her throat. He had called her back into the world, out of the safe refuge in which she had hidden herself. He had violated the principles of protecting and guiding by which she had lived for ten years. He was dangerous, and he had involved them all in danger. He would do so again. She watched him stride off to face that danger and knew that she loved him.

* * * *

Ashton had been stabbed by an assailant who knew his or her business. His body lay on a table in an anteroom at the back of Hardwicke House while Charles waited for a constable Goldsworthy trusted. The marchioness had disappeared. She had had Charles's measure from the first. Hers had been the grand design. He meant to distract her with flowered waistcoats and gallantry, but it was she who had seen his weakness and distracted him by embroiling Octavia in her schemes. Now she would make her move against her real target. He still did not know where she would strike, but before he could stop her, he had to find Octavia.

He returned to Dover Street before dawn and received a chilling message.

You can prevent your sister's ruin if you are willing to meet me when and where I shall direct you. Any delay, any involvement of other parties, and she will be lost to you forever.

In Octavia's hand—or a hand that closely resembled hers—was scrawled the added note—

Charles, I implore you, please do as our cousin says. I am wholly in the captain's power.

*Though it is a rare occurrence, it must be said that on
occasion a woman in possession of that peculiarly feminine gift
for noting and reflecting upon her feelings may yet misread the
state of her heart. She has perhaps studied to be collected and
calm, and from the long habit of subduing unwise feelings, does
not recognize how sincerely attached to her a gentleman has
become and how necessary to her happiness he is. In such a
case, only the direst threat of the loss of his presence in her life
is likely to awaken her to the true nature of her feelings.*

—The Husband Hunter's Guide to London

Chapter 20

The day dawned clear and cold after the snow of the evening before.
Harriet, looking out her window, watched Mars rise in the east in a sky
as deep blue as the shawl she had envied in the arcade shop. She had not
slept. Her letter of resignation, addressed to Lady Luxborough, lay on
her little writing desk. The borrowed ball gown had been restored to her
ladyship's wardrobe. Harriet's packed bag stood by the door. No word had
come from Wynford.

Through the whole of their acquaintance, she had had before her evidence
of his true intentions. She, who prided herself on clear-headedness, had
allowed sentiments and sensations to cloud her judgment. His attentions
had seemed sincere even in the face of those appalling waistcoats, which
she now knew signaled where his true purpose lay. Attaching her regard
had been an accident. The mistletoe had been to blame, an unfortunate
consequence of Jasper's fall from the tree and Harriet's foolish hanging
of the boy's trophy in the second-best drawing room.

She laid her hand on the cool paper of her letter, as if she could feel its
sense and logic. Resolutions made in the heat of strong feeling were harder
to keep when they required action. But she knew, as she hoped Octavia
would discover about Gresham, that one could not cut out a hurt the way
surgeons could cut out a tumor, and that changing oneself, one's hair
and face and clothes, even one's manner of speaking or moving, did not
distance one from pain. But changing one's place, the very scenery of one's
daily life, could lessen the power of memory. Harriet had done it before,
and she could do it again. She straightened her shoulders. Through the

window, Mars glittered brightly. If only she could change the sky. Perhaps in one of the great manufacturing cities, the smoke of the mills would hide the stars, and some family, rising in gentility in the world, would need a governess. Lady Luxborough might wish for Harriet to accept Wynford, but she would not be so unkind as to withhold a letter of introduction.

A whimper and a scratch at her door reminded her that before she could change her life she must walk the dog.

* * * *

Charles stumbled into Goldsworthy's office as the sky lightened. His captor's pistol scraped the side of his head as he righted himself and came to a halt. The man, who spoke with the language and accents of London's rookeries, had earlier relieved Charles of his coat and wallet.

There was no sign of Octavia. It made him hope that the plot against her had been a ruse after all, the message a forgery, to entrap him.

His gaze took in the disarray: canvas curtains pulled down, glass-fronted cabinets broken open, maps ripped from the walls, and papers spilling from file drawers. Perry, coatless like Charles, sat bound, gagged and shaking in one of the green leather chairs. In his battered face with its blackened eyes and swollen, bloodied mouth, his eyes flashed both warning and entreaty. Charles's gaze flicked from Perry to Goldsworthy. The big man lay slumped over his desk, his huge hands splayed over the documents there, as if he could shield them with his fallen bulk. Under his shaggy locks a small pool of blood stained his papers. They had thought him indestructible, like a mighty oak, or like the Green Man of legend who one Christmastide invited a knight from Arthur's court to cut off his head. When Gawain swung the axe, the Green Man simply picked up his severed head and rode away. Goldsworthy was mortal after all. Charles tasted failure. He had protected neither his sister nor his friends.

Standing over Goldsworthy, pistol in gloved hand, was the marchioness, her face flushed with triumph. She wore a heavy dark cloak and chinchilla fur hat. Charles's mind went to work instantly. She had two accomplices, the man with the pistol to Charles's head and a fellow rifling through Goldsworthy's cabinets, tossing papers into an open valise on the floor. The odds were unpromising, but there would be a weakness somewhere in his opponent.

"Good morning, Lord Wynford," she said. "You've stumbled into a tragedy. Your friend Mr. Goldsworthy is bankrupt, you see. He's failed to revive the club into which he sank his fortune. There was no gentlemanly way out for him, alas, but to take his own life."

Charles said nothing. His mind went on calculating distances and odds. "I almost gave up on finding this nest of vipers. My friend in Paris did not wish to believe that such an operation existed, a club for gentlemen spies run by a rude, rustic mountain of flesh." She shrugged. "Now your Goldsworthy will no longer trouble us."

"How did a London merchant trading in coffee trouble your friend?" Charles asked blandly.

The marchioness laughed a short, dry laugh. She pointed her pistol at Perry. "Your friend has been most inconvenient, seeking to know more than he should about me, but your sister told me it was Mr. Pilkington who kept you in those waistcoats. So I watched him. How intriguing that he went in and came out of a chemist's shop on Bond Street with a waistcoat.

"Naturally, I am curious about this shop, but it is not a true shop, is it? More like a bit of scenery on a stage managed by a mere child. It is when one goes behind the red velvet curtain that one finds the old man's tailoring room and the path through a garden to this...club."

Charles made himself meet the marchioness's gaze. The pieces of the puzzle had come together. Goldsworthy and the club itself had been her target all along. Charles tried not to think of Miranda and old Kirby. It was possible that they were beyond his help. But Perry was not, and he could not be sure that Goldsworthy was dead. If Wilde had escaped the trap, help might arrive. First, he had to find out whether the marchioness had Octavia.

"You don't have Octavia, do you?" He stepped further into the room, almost close enough to reach Perry. The man with the pistol followed, keeping the steel mouth of the gun against Charles's head.

The marchioness's smile widened with satisfaction. "She's ruined. Fanshaw will see to it."

Charles made himself answer carelessly. "I doubt it. Fanshaw is not Ashton. He's a calculating sort of fellow. He won't risk his position over a woman with friends in high places."

"Friends in high places?" Her laugh was bitter. "When has that ever protected a woman? She was most helpful, your sister, so artless, so trusting, so willing to share her little confidences."

Charles kept his face impassive. It was plain that the marchioness had no more use for Octavia. "You never meant to establish yourself in London, did you?" he asked. He saw her plan more clearly now. She was a break in the Russian pattern. In the past the Russians had used agents like the charming Count Malikov, who had spent years moving in the highest ranks of London society while recruiting its members to pass along English secrets. The club had been England's defense against such men. Charles understood now that the marchioness had been sent to destroy the club itself.

The only advantage to their side that he could see lay in her mood. He noted the flush in her cheeks, the glitter in her eyes, and her loose hold on the pistol. She was in the grip of triumph, a curious and untrustworthy emotion. It made one feel quite unconquerable, while one's foe appeared helpless, crushed beneath one's boot heel. By a strange paradox the defeat of an enemy left one hungry for more. She was dressed for travel, for escape, and yet she lingered—caught in the heady rush of her success. If he had any chance of disarming her, it would have to be before her mood changed.

He lowered his gaze to the big man's slumped figure and counted the guns in the room. If the marchioness had shot Goldsworthy, she would need to reload. The man with the pistol to Charles's head would have one shot. The man rifling the cabinets must have another. The guns in the cabinets would not be loaded, but the swords were ready for use. He needed only a diversion.

Goldsworthy's right thumb twitched.

* * * *

Harriet, dressed for travel, let Cat lead the way. It would be a farewell outing, a leave-taking of the neighborhood. Cat headed south through ankle-deep snow, crunching a path through the powdery drifts, shaking his paws every now and then, and lifting his nose in the air to catch a scent. Smoke rose from dozens of chimneys. Servants shoveled walkways, and an old man, his donkey sending steaming breath into the air, his cart mounded with holly and mistletoe, his face and head swathed in a long green scarf, stood negotiating with a housekeeper at a kitchen door over a basket of green branches and bright red berries. Another Christmas was nearly come, and Harriet could peer in the windows of London to see it as she passed.

She stroked the donkey's nose, and the holly man called after her.

"Miss, 'ave a branch of 'olly."

Harriet started to shake her head, but the man whistled, and Cat came to him. He tucked a short bough in Cat's collar. "Merry Christmas, miss," he said, holding out a sprig of mistletoe.

Harriet took it, laughing. The stuff was inescapable. She stuck the sprig in the ribbon of her sober gray bonnet.

"Merry Christmas, sir." She could not help replying. She dropped Cat's lead and reached for a coin from her reticule, but the holly man waved her off and mounted his cart.

She turned to follow Cat, who had reached a familiar corner. There was no danger in it today. Wynford, the spy, was off in pursuit of his enemy. Cat kept going. There was no hurry. Today the rest of the Luxborough staff would leave for the country. She would send her letter of resignation with them and summon a hack for a posting house and the north, where she was sure she would find her next employment.

She was fixing this resolution in her mind when they reached Albemarle Street. The austere and regular yellow stone façade of the Royal Institution dominated the street. With a pang, she realized that it was a part of her London life that she would miss. In front of the building, Cat halted and lifted his quivering nose to catch a scent, his body tense with awareness. Abruptly, he bounded toward Piccadilly, indifferent to Harriet's calls. At the odd canvas-shrouded building Octavia and Harriet had remarked on days earlier, Cat darted under a large gray flapping canvas and disappeared.

"Oh, Cat, not today," Harriet cried. She quickened her step. Wynford could not be there, of course. He was off in pursuit of Octavia or the marchioness or Fanshaw. She didn't know. When she reached the building, she could hear the dog's deep-voiced howl receding into the interior.

She ducked under the canvas and found a great door standing open on a vast empty marble foyer from which a grand staircase rose. Somewhere up the stairs, Cat's howls echoed.

* * * *

Charles recognized the dog's howls instantly. There was no mistaking the deep-voiced baying. The surprise was that the unholy sound came from within the club as the cries came up the stairs and into the passageway. Charles had thought his failure complete, but he was wrong. Cat was leading Harriet Swanley into the marchioness's trap. His enemy's face changed at the first howl, her mood of triumph vanishing in cunning wariness. Her grip on the pistol instantly tightened. Charles saw his advantage vanish.

The marchioness spoke in rapid bursts to her two accomplices. The man holding Charles shoved him forward toward Perry. The fellow at the files left them and closed the valise and dropped it by the door. He crossed to Goldsworthy's desk and removed the glass from the lamp.

A heavy thud shook the door. Cat's howl filled the room.

"Apparently, we must part sooner than I expected." The marchioness stood at the corner of the big desk, beside Goldsworthy's slumped body. "The tragedy, you understand, must deepen. You English like a good Christmas fire, do you not? Mr. Goldsworthy, you see, set fire to his office, and you and your friend, coming to his aid, were consumed in the flames."

She nodded to the man in front of the desk. He tipped over the lamp. The papers at the edge of the desk blackened and smoked, a small flame danced above the curling paper.

Perry strained against the bonds that held him in the chair.

A second crash shook the door. The howling became frantic. The pistol at Charles's head wobbled slightly. "Wot beast is that?" asked Charles's captor, glancing over his shoulder.

"The beast's name is Catapult," Charles said.

"It's just a dog, you fool," said the marchioness.

The door shuddered under a third blow. Then it opened. The dog hurled himself at the man holding Charles, knocking him to the floor. The man shrieked and writhed, tangled in Charles's greatcoat, trying to cover his face with his arms. Cat pinned him down, snarling and tearing at the coat. The pistol went flying, discharging a bullet into the molding at the base of the wall.

The marchioness ignored her henchman, looking over Charles's shoulder. "Ah," she said, "Miss Milk and Water. You are just in time to join the tragedy."

Charles turned to the door as Harriet Swanley entered the room. He saw at once how wrong the marchioness was about his love. Harriet Swanley was a woman of pearls and steel. She appeared breathless from the stairs, but her remarkable gray eyes were as clear-headed as ever. With a glance, she surveyed the scene. Then her gaze, wry and resolute, met his. Her eyes declared that she understood his part in leading them to this moment, and she loved him in defiance of sense and self-interest.

She offered the marchioness a steady, fearless smile. "I take it you've been exposed," she said, stepping boldly forward and reaching up to untie the strings of her gray bonnet. Charles noted the mistletoe stuck in the band of ribbon on her hat.

"You had a French governess, perhaps," Harriet continued. "A woman who ate *frippe* and taught you her maxims. You thought you could use her past to create the fictional marchioness from Saumur who had a family tie to the Davenhams."

"Miss Swanley," Charles said, "may I present Russian agent Sophia Dashkova."

"You English, so little understanding of the world beyond your tiny island."

"And yet," said Harriet, "we are able to unmask an imposter."

"Get the dog off me," cried the man on the floor, still pinned under Cat. Dashkova turned to her accomplice at the desk. "Get rid of the dog," she snapped.

The man looked at her and at Cat, who continued to shake his head, snarling and tearing at the fallen man's clothes, his body resting on the man's chest. The standing man shoved Cat with his boot, but the dog only growled more fiercely and did not budge.

"Useless," the marchioness declared. "Turn your gun on Pilkington." She put her pistol on the edge of the desk and removed her gloves. With unhurried calm she took up the gun and began to reload. "Do not move, Wynford, or your friend dies."

"Now or later is not much of a bargain." Charles moved a pace closer to Perry.

Dashkova's hands paused briefly, then she finished loading and pointed her pistol at Charles. "You are tiresome, you English," she said. "Now we must finish."

The fire on the desk had died down to smoking bits of charred paper. Dashkova made a little sound of disgust.

"Not enough bullets to put everyone away," said Charles. "You might want to flee instead. Ashton's death is known. The authorities will be here soon."

Dashkova looked around, making some calculation. It was the first sign of hesitation he'd seen in her.

"Shoot the dog," she ordered.

The man pointing his gun at Peregrine stared at her, uncomprehending.

"Cat!" Charles called. The dog instantly lifted his head and looked at Charles. "To Harry," he ordered.

The dog bounded to Harriet, who knelt down to take him in her arms.

"You English and your dogs." Dashkova laughed. "Very well then." She raised her pistol.

Charles stepped into the path of the gun.

At that moment Goldsworthy groaned. Dashkova's gaze flicked to him. Charles pulled Perry's chair, toppling Perry onto the man trying to rise from the floor.

Dashkova fired.

The bullet's fiery trail grazed Charles's side as Goldsworthy heaved up from the desk, flinging one huge hand backward, catching Dashkova in the chest and knocking her against the wall.

Her head hit the paneling with a crack. Her fur hat slipped down over her eyes as she slid to the floor. Her accomplice remained holding his pistol pointed at Charles, but his gaze swung to the door.

Voices came up hollowly from below, urgently calling Charles's name. Footsteps pounded toward them. Wilde burst into the room, followed by Octavia and John Jowers.

The man with the gun saw that the advantage had shifted. He kept the gun pointed at Charles and burst into speech. "This b'aint the lay we was promised. I won't be lagged for nicking a bleeding coat." As he spoke, his gaze drifted toward the door. Abruptly, he bolted straight into a fist thrown by John Jowers. The punch knocked the man out cold.

Goldsworthy leaned on his great desk, his shaggy locks matted with blood. "Well done, all," he said and sank down heavily into his chair.

When one has been wounded in the course of life, it is easy to believe that holding on to one's secret anger and persisting in one's sense of grievance is a form of strength. Nothing could be further from the truth. The ability to love after setbacks and disappointments does not come naturally to us but must be cultivated lest we fall into a state of resentment fatal to all our future happiness.

—*The Husband Hunter's Guide to London*

Chapter 21

The gun's report in her ears and acrid smoke in her nose, Harriet stumbled to her feet and reached for Wynford. He seized her in a crushing embrace. Strong arms held her against a hard, warm, living body. She wrapped her arms around him, returning his fierce hold. The small black mouth of the pistol had pointed directly at him, a circle of nothingness, and he had stepped in front of it.

She pulled back in his embrace and hit him once on the chest with a fist. "I could have lost you. You stood in front of Cat."

"I could have lost you," he corrected, looking solemnly down at her. "I stood in front of you."

Her ears cleared. She was dimly aware of noise and movement around her. "You are not hurt?" she asked.

He grinned at her. "You wore mistletoe in your bonnet. Were you coming to find me?"

"I was leaving London. I meant only to give Cat one last walk. He... Well, you know how he is about finding you." She stepped out of his arms, and her glove came away covered in blood. "Oh, you are hurt." She pulled off the ruined glove and pushed aside his coat to press her palm against the blood welling up from a long gash in his purple waistcoat.

"My love," he said. "Let me release Perry. Then you can tend to me all you wish." Wynford reached down and righted Perry's chair and began to undo his bonds. "I'm sorry I got you into this, my friend."

"It's my fault," Perry said in a broken voice. "Those waistcoats were my idea, and they never fooled her for a moment. And then..." Perry hung his head. "I led her right to you."

"Rubbish, my friend," Charles said gently. "You did more to unmask her than I did. Now sit here until we can get a surgeon to look at your face."

Harriet inwardly applauded her love's good sense. A surgeon was needed. She looked around to see whom they could send.

John Jowers stood over the unconscious would-be robber, holding the man's own pistol. Charles handed Perry's loosened bonds to Wilde, who sprang forward and tied up Cat's victim and dragged him to a corner. The youth then turned to the big man behind the desk. The russet-haired giant appeared clear-headed in spite of his bleeding head.

"Kirby and Miranda?" he asked Wilde.

"Safe," Wilde assured him. "What do we do with her?"

Wilde carefully approached the fallen Dashkova.

"She breathes," Wilde announced. He kicked her pistol away from her side.

"She could still be armed," the big man warned.

"Her right arm looks crooked. It may be broken." Wilde gently lifted the fur hat from over her face.

Her eyes opened, narrow slits of pain and rage.

"Can you stand?" Wilde asked.

She let out a torrent of words in what Harriet surmised must be her own tongue, the hatred in them unmistakable.

Wilde offered her a hand to rise, ignoring her attempts to kick and claw at him. She stood for an instant on her own and spat at the big man. Then her legs folded, and with a groan she sank to the floor again.

Charles strode forward, taking a position behind her. At his nod, Wilde secured her feet while Charles lifted from under her arms.

Guessing their intention, Harriet swept the huge desk of burnt and bloodstained papers. Dashkova groaned and lapsed into a faint as Charles and Wilde laid her down.

"She's no cousin of ours, is she, Charles?" Octavia asked. "What will become of her?"

Charles turned Dashkova's face to one side, examining the wound to the back of her head. "If she wants to live, transportation is her only chance. If we imprison her in England, her Russian colleagues will quickly find a way to silence her."

"Oh Charles," Octavia said. "You never got my message."

"Doesn't matter. You're safe." He put an arm around his sister, his eyes closing briefly, and Harriet worked to subdue her impatience that his wound should go untreated. She saw him differently now. He was a warrior in spite of his absurd waistcoats, a man who would protect his own whatever the cost.

"Forgive me," Octavia mumbled against his side. "I sent a message as soon as I could. To tell you I was safe and the marchioness was a fraud. I heard her talking, you see, to Captain Fanshaw. He said I was a bird that had flown and he couldn't help her. She said he had proved worthless, unable to seduce a peahen." Octavia paused for breath. "I knew then that I was being used. Fanshaw had taken my cloak, so I talked my way into a lady's carriage. She gave me a great scold, but she took me to Mr. Jowers's house, where he lives with his Aunt Louisa."

Charles glanced across the top of her head to acknowledge his gratitude to John Jowers.

The sound of more voices and footsteps, male and authoritative, rose from the stairs. A small, round-faced man strode into the room at the head of five scarlet-coated soldiers. The gentleman wore gold-rimmed spectacles as round as his bald, freckled head and emitted a palpable air of importance and command.

His frowning gaze took in the room's disorder and settled on the big man behind the desk. "Goldsworthy, I've always distrusted your methods. Too bloody by half. I warned you, you could be shut down."

"So you did, Lord Chartwell," Goldsworthy replied with unimpaired cordiality. "Look what we've got for you this fine morning—Sophia Dashkova. Straight from Zovsky she comes. A bold baggage she is."

Charles cleared his throat, and Chartwell's gaze swung to him. "Last night she murdered Major Ashton, sir."

Chartwell took in the information but returned to his earlier theme. "How the devil did she find you out?" he asked Goldsworthy. "No one knows you exist except a few drudges in the Exchequer."

"Would one of those drudges be Edenhorn, sir?" Charles asked mildly. "Edenhorn has been one of Dashkova's admirers from the beginning."

When Chartwell showed every sign of continuing his attack on Goldsworthy, Harriet could stand it no longer. "Pardon me, gentlemen," she said. "Can assessing the full measure of blame wait until a surgeon is summoned to tend to the wounded?"

Chartwell's face changed as he took in Goldsworthy's matted hair, Perry's battered face, and the blood staining Charles's trouser leg. "Right," he said, and fired off a series of orders to the soldiers who accompanied him. Instantly, a man was dispatched to summon a surgeon. Two soldiers seized Dashkova's accomplices and marched them away while two other men took a plank from the bare scaffolding in the room to serve as a litter on which to carry the fallen agent.

With very little bustle, the ransacked room was emptied of the enemy. Goldsworthy turned to Wilde. "Lad, get our wounded to more comfortable accommodations. We'll have the surgeon here in no time." The big man turned back to Chartwell. "Let's talk."

* * * *

The sky was bright outside the club by the time the surgeon finished cleaning and dressing the wound in Wynford's side. Dr. Ryle was a brisk, efficient practitioner of his craft who did his work with precision and dispatch. With his departure, Octavia and John Jowers left as well, taking the dog and intending to offer their support to Perry before returning to John's aunt.

After hours of uncertainty and danger in the midst of friends and enemies alike, Harriet was alone with her love in the full knowledge that she loved him unreservedly. The tiny spark of awareness that had first glowed in her girlhood when he took the trouble to seek a remedy for his ailing servant had never gone out. If she had not been distracted by and determined to resist his very real attractions, she would have observed that at every encounter with him since he had asked her to help Octavia the little spark had grown until now it blazed brightly.

Under lowered lids she regarded him now in the privacy of the comfortable gentleman's suite to which Wilde had led them. It was a male setting, and it suited him. She and Octavia had quickly stripped away his bloodstained neckcloth and jacket, waistcoat and fine lawn shirt. The doctor had, as a last step in his procedures, wrapped a bandage around Wynford's waist and written a set of instructions for Harriet, entrusting his care to her.

Sitting in a mahogany armchair, bloodied and bandaged, his face drawn and wearied, dressed only in his trousers, he took her breath away. She had been used to finding beauty in the distant stars, but now she saw that the most ordinary things of earth shone as brightly when one truly loved them. She let her gaze touch the knob of his wrist and the fine hair dusting the back of his hand, the curve of muscle in his languid arm, and his proud, straight shoulders. Her gaze found and touched the hollow arc of his torso, curved in the chair like a slice of new moon in the sky. And though she merely looked, she discovered a hunger she had not known one could have, the hunger for skin against skin. It left her shaken, aware of just how ungovernable her passion for him might become.

Her gaze reached his face and met his still-troubled one.

"Are you in pain?" she asked. The doctor had given him a draught. "I never meant for you or Octavia to be in any danger," he confessed. "I thought I was cleverer than Dashkova and ahead of her every step of the way. Arrogant of me, I know. I didn't see how she was the one leading me where she wanted me to go. Even after she murdered Ashton, I did not recognize that her purpose all along was to destroy the club."

Harriet moved and knelt at his feet, needing to touch him and resting her hands on the bloodstained knees of his trousers. She offered no words yet, only her touch while he unburdened his heart.

"I think my mother must have felt the same way. She must have believed that we were in no danger from her mission, that she could protect us." He paused, his eyes blank, his attention inward on the past that only he could see. "The agony of her death must have been the greater for not knowing whether her sacrifice was enough."

Harriet laid her head on his knees, and after a moment he lifted a hand to cup her head. She willed him to believe that facing Dashkova's bullet absolved him of the errors and failings he claimed for himself.

"Our mother," he said, "has been the Christmas ghost that's haunted Wynford Hall since Octavia was a babe."

Once more he seemed to lose himself in thought, then began again. "I met your brother at the ball," he said. "I should never have left that day. You would not have suffered from his cruelty and greed."

She lifted her head and gave him her most quelling glance. "You must not blame yourself for my brother's sins. You did not know who I was."

"I'm sorry about Nelson," he said.

"He told you?"

He nodded. "Boasted of it."

She whacked her palm against his chest. "And that's why you stepped in front of a bullet?"

He grabbed her hand and held it to his heart. "I could not let Dashkova shoot your dog, for Cat is your dog, you know."

She smiled up at him, struggling against the sting of tears in her eyes. "Oh, I think he's your dog," she said.

His hand framed her face. "Our dog now." He grabbed the chair arms to push himself to his feet.

Harriet rocked back on her knees. "Where do you think you're going?"

"There's a great deal to do," he said, but his eyes glazed over as the draught took effect.

Harriet stood and offered a shoulder for support, sliding an arm around his waist. "First, bed, my lor—"

"You must call me Charles," he said, looking down at her with laughter in his eyes. He glanced across the room at the large, comfortable bed. "Join me."

Together they crossed the room. Harriet turned back the counterpane and helped him stretch out on his uninjured side. She unlaced her half boots and climbed up beside him, and he settled her against the curve of his body.

Just when she thought he had drifted off, he spoke once more. "Remind me to tell you very soon how much I have been looking forward to taking you to bed."

The husband hunter who has guarded her heart and maintained her reserve until certain of an equal return of love may now, when all suspense is over, delight in an open exchange of those feelings and promises which are the sure foundation of her future happiness.

—*The Husband Hunter's Guide to London*

Chapter 22

Harriet stood at the drawing room window of the Davenhams' London townhouse, looking out on the Christmas Eve dusk. Light from the candles behind her made a pale white square on the walkway and caught a few glittering snowflakes in its glow as they fell. She smiled at her own shadow outlined in that square of light, like her old self outside in the darkness. She shivered a little at the cold from the window, but she did not mind it, not now when she had traded places with that other Harriet.

In the distance coming nearer she could hear the sound of a band of Waits, London's rude minstrels with their rustic horns and drum, offering their carols to the neighborhood for a few coins. She tried to catch the tune but heard only the thump of the drum. Behind her Octavia and John Jowers matched wits playfully as they worked on some project Octavia said was necessary to the Christmas celebration. On a rug by the hearth, an unstirring Catapult looked most unworthy of his name. Only his ears twitched a little in his dreams. He still wore the sprig of holly in his collar. She did not know where Charles had got to, only that he had claimed he had things to do for Christmas and that he would be back.

In the two days since the confrontation with Sophia Dashkova, they had only been apart while Charles tended to the unpleasant business of Dashkova's imprisonment and the happier matter of their future. Harriet had to admire his efficiency. Her days as a governess were over. Lady Luxborough had been notified by express of the change in her situation, and a return express had brought congratulations.

Charles had moved both Harriet and John Jowers's Aunt Louisa into his house. His solicitors were at work negotiating settlements with Harriet's brother over an inheritance he had long withheld from her. Charles had even called upon her mother, and there was hope of a reconciliation. In time Harriet would see her. Octavia had given Harriet the little blue

Husband Hunter's Guide to London book, and Harriet had passed the time of Charles's absence in reading it, surprised to discover how much wisdom it contained. The passages about true happiness seemed to her the wisest of all. She wondered if it was possible to be drunk on happiness.

In return Harriet had given her copy of Emilie du Chatelet's *Discourses on Happiness* to Octavia, a woman newly freed to be herself and find her own happiness.

Harriet and Charles had spent the two nights talking by the fire, Cat at their feet. It had been necessary to touch and kiss. Each had confessed the steps by which he or she had progressed from awareness to admiration to love. The stages had to be analyzed.

"I'm an analyst," he told her. "It's what I do."

"It was the mistletoe that first alerted me to my altered feelings," he admitted. "Seeing you under it was a constant temptation."

"It was those waistcoats that misled me so much about your true character," she revealed. "But they made me jealous, as well. I knew every time I saw you in persimmon or stripes or red or purple that you would be meeting her."

He laughed a rueful laugh. "I confused the wrong woman," he said. And she told him wordlessly how unconfused she now was.

Tonight they would be a houseful for Christmas Eve, Octavia and John Jowers, his Aunt Louisa and Perry, and Harriet and Charles. The holly man had come again, and boughs bedecked the mantel and sconces. Jasper's mistletoe had been retrieved from the Luxboroughs' second-best drawing room and hung from the chandelier in the entry.

The sound of the Waits came nearer. Harriet heard their familiar "Fa la la la la, la la la la." The snow fell more thickly now. And there was Charles at the head of the band of four musicians, in motley coats, hats, and scarves. He spoke to their leader, a man in a round-crowned white hat with a big drum hanging from a strap round his neck. Then he glanced up at Harriet and waved. Harriet waved back, and the musicians began to play their oldest song, a song Harriet had rarely heard since her childhood with a refrain that came back to her at once—*Past three o'clock, And a cold frosty morning, Past three a clock; Good morrow, masters all!*

Cat stirred at the sound and came to her side. She gave his silky ears a rub. When the drawing room door opened, the dog slipped away, and Harriet smiled, knowing without turning round that Charles was there.

She heard the others greet him, and then his voice came low and close, "Harry, you're cold, my love."

His hands closed around her shoulders, and she leaned back against him with a smile. His cheek against hers was cold, and she trembled a little in his hold. They stood in that lightest of embraces, her shoulders against his chest, cheek-to-cheek, as the song ended. The drummer beat his drum again, and the Waits marched away.

"Come up to the roof," Charles invited.

She turned to face him, laughing. "What a contradictory fellow you are. You said I was cold."

"A good thing, too. For else I fear my gift to you would be to no purpose." He gave her shoulders a squeeze and stepped back to reach for a package tied in brown paper and string. She glanced at him. He led her to an armchair, and when she sat, he settled the soft, light package in her lap. She pulled away the string and unfolded the paper, and her breath caught. There was the blue shawl she'd admired in the arcade.

"Thank you," she said.

"I wanted you to have it," he said simply. "At the time I could not have said why. Now I know."

She lifted the shawl from the paper. It was as blue as she remembered, and softer than she had imagined. He helped her to her feet and arranged the thing around her shoulders. "I'll wait to tell you how I hope to see you wear it one day."

A flash of awareness coursed through her as hotly as any electric current. She felt her cheeks go up in flame.

"Now," he said in a rasp of a voice, "the roof. There's a constellation I want to show you."

"There are no stars tonight," she said, recovering a little.

"Are you sure?" He took her hand and pulled her along.

Octavia and John looked up at them. "Oh, are you going? You should see what we've done." Octavia rose and stepped back from the table. There stood an oaken ark, three stories high with a hinged roof that lifted, and one side open with partitions for the animals. Octavia and John had arranged the painted pairs of carved animals in the stalls with giraffes on the top floor, and lions, cows, and camels on the bottom, sheep and elephants in the middle. Octavia had brightened the ark with sprigs of holly and berries.

"I brought it from home," Octavia said. "It would not be Christmas if we did not put up the ark, Charles."

Harriet gave Charles's hand a quick squeeze. Octavia, too, had come in from the cold for Christmas.

"Pardon us," said Charles, tugging Harriet's hand. "We've some stargazing to do."

"There won't be any stars tonight," said John with a puzzled look.

"You never know," said Charles. "Don't let my sister lead you into any mischief," he warned.

"Go," said Louisa Jowers placidly, looking up from her book. "They are safe with me. I'll see that they don't come to blows."

"Come to blows!" Octavia protested with a laugh.

Harriet smiled. John Jowers might not know it yet, but Octavia was his, or would be very soon. Charles pulled Harriet away, out the door, past the hall table where he took up a lamp to the stairs.

"The old schoolroom," he said simply, "has a door that opens onto the roof."

She nodded, gathering her skirts and pulling her new shawl tightly around her.

Up and up they went until they came to a door under the eaves.

He turned to her with a solemn look. "Now you must close your eyes and trust me."

She obeyed, and he opened the door and handed her out into the snowy London night. Flakes swirled around her, softly touching her face and melting. His grip on her shoulders steadied her.

"Ready?" he asked.

She nodded and opened her eyes. On a small platform stood two score or more candles in shining glass vases arranged to form a message.

"MARRY ME," the candles said.

"I love you, Harry," he said, his voice deep in a way she was coming to know signaled his desire for her. "It's our own constellation, for the darkest nights."

She turned in his arms and looked up into the face she'd come to love. "Yes," she said, and he crushed her to him, her love who gave her the earth and the stars. They lingered on the roof, storing up kisses and touches before descending to their first Christmas feast.

Later, leaning together on a sofa, after the dinner, after the games and pudding and merriment, with the house quiet once again, the fire still burning, the dog at their feet, he offered one last gift, a piece of paper.

As she looked at it in the dim light, he explained, "It's a special license. We can marry tomorrow."

"Very wise, I think," she said, a little breathless, thinking that if he meant to see her in just her blue shawl, she meant to see him in just his blue dressing gown.

"Merry Christmas, my love," he said.

"Merry Christmas," she replied.

Epilogue

Nate Wilde, his head tipped back, his hands in his pockets, studied the façade of the building on Albemarle Street that had been his home for nearly three years. He was twenty-one, a child of Bread Street in one of London's darkest rookeries. He had lost homes before and not regretted them as he rose in the world. So he wondered at himself that he should have a heavy heart at seeing Goldsworthy's spy club close.

He had never seen the building without the scaffolding and canvas that had concealed the building's true purpose from the eyes of ordinary Londoners. Until the French marchioness, who was really the Russian agent Sophia Dashkova, no one outside the members of a most exclusive spy club had guessed that from inside the building the wiliest of spymasters had run his network of agents and informers.

They were all there for the building's unveiling—the first three spies, Blackstone, Hazelwood, and Clare; Lynley and his bride Lady Emily, the only lady spy; and Wynford, who had lately saved the club and its precious files from total destruction. Standing beside the spies, his lads, as he called them, was Samuel Goldsworthy himself, the towering giant who ran the place, and old Kirby, and his daughter Miranda, whom Nate would marry soon.

Miranda slipped her hand in his, his proud shop girl with the airs of a lady.

It was Twelfth Night, the final day of Christmas, and the sun was as blinding as the January air was crisp and cold. They had stepped outside after viewing the transformation of the interior. Goldsworthy shook every man's hand, except Nate's, and thanked them all for their service to king and country. That was all right. The club was to become a legitimate gentleman's club now, and Nate had been offered the position of majordomo, if he wanted it. He didn't know where he stood on the offer. If he took it, he would be able to marry Miranda with no further delay.

Yet the idea didn't sit well with him. He didn't think he would like supplying ordinary gentlemen with superior coffee and sandwiches, or looking after their coats and hats, and answering their questions or meeting their requests when it wasn't for a case, when he had no chance to be involved. Miranda had told him she would accept whatever decision he made. She and her father, who ran the shop on Bond Street that was actually a front for a rear entrance to the club, would give up that establishment and move to a more modest street, her father no longer wishing to manage a shop.

Miranda gave his hand another squeeze. "Everyone's leaving," she whispered. "It's too cold to idle about here."

He roused himself from his thoughts to say proper farewells and accept everyone's wishes for the new year. Miranda, with a brief glance at him, took her father's arm to help him back inside. In a few minutes only Nate and Goldsworthy stood on the pavement.

The big man laid one of his heavy tree-branch arms across Nate's shoulders. "Well, lad," he began, "I take it you don't fancy being majordomo when the club changes."

Nate swallowed. The moment to choose had come. "It wouldn't be the same, sir," he said.

"No, it wouldn't," Goldsworthy agreed. Yet his heavy arm still rested on Nate's shoulders. There would be more coming. Nate waited. "I've been thinking," the big man went on. "I doubt Dashkova, fiendish woman, is the end of it for the Russians. Zovsky or his masters will regroup and throw something new at us before this new year is very old."

Nate held his breath. Goldsworthy had something in mind after all.

"So, tomorrow, I think, you and I must start looking for a new home for our little enterprise. What do you say to that, lad?" Goldsworthy lifted his arm from Nate's shoulders.

Nate looked up grinning. "Yes, sir," he said, his heart light.

About the Author

Photo Credit: Loren Moore

Kate Moore is a former English teacher and three-time RITA finalist, Golden Heart, and Book Buyers Best Award winner. She writes Austen inspired fiction set in 19th Century England or contemporary California. Her heroes are men of courage, competence, and unmistakable virility, with determination so strong it keeps their sensuality in check until they meet the right woman. Her heroines take on the world with practical good sense and kindness to bring those heroes into a circle of love and family. Sometimes there's even a dog. Kate lives north of San Francisco with her surfer husband, their yellow Lab, a Pack 'n Play for visiting grandbabies, and miles of crowded bookshelves. Kate's family and friends offer endless support and humor. Her children are her best works, and her husband is her favorite hero. Visit Kate at Facebook.com/KateMooreAuthor or contact her at kate@katemoore.com.

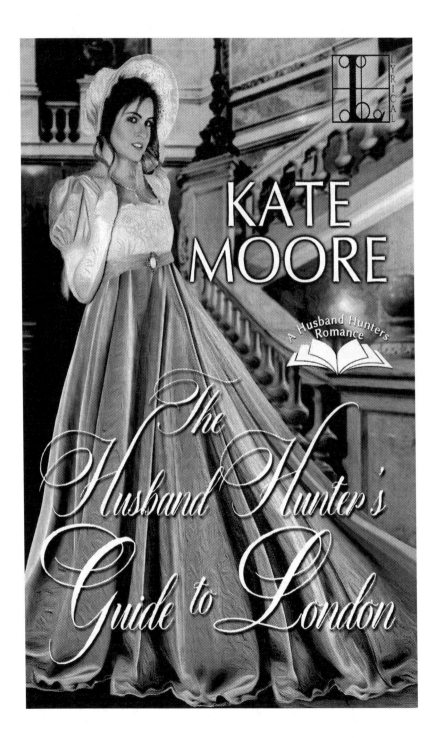

KATE
MOORE

The
Husband Hunter's
Guide to London

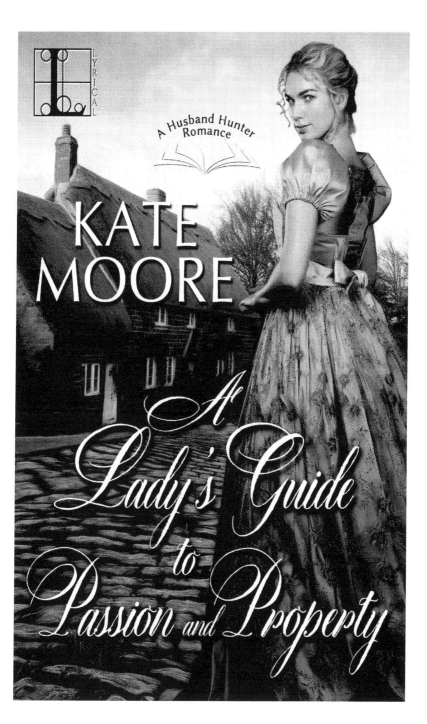

A Husband Hunter
Romance

KATE
MOORE

A
Lady's Guide
to
Passion and Property

KATE MOORE

A Spy's Guide to Seduction

A Husband Hunter Romance

Printed in the United States
by Baker & Taylor Publisher Services